MEDICINE AND MURDER

THE HEMLOCK INN MYSTERIES BOOK 3

JOSEPHINE SMITH

Dear reader,
I hope you enjoy Simone's
story. I live down the
street, and I'm so happy
to share this book with
you. Happy Reading!
Josephine

WESTERN COAST PRESS

To Sadie and Mindy,
for all the cuddles and pets.

1

I held in a sneeze as the clock struck noon. Moments later, the sneeze ricocheted through me without warning, shooting pain coursing down my back in response. I groaned, resting my head against the cupboard I was kneeling under. Fortunately, no one was in the lobby with me, so I was safe from prying eyes.

"Simone, what are you doing?"

I jerked in surprise, banging my head against the cupboard and sending another spasm down my back. I shut my eyes tight, taking deep breaths as the wave of pain passed.

"Don't scare me like that," I said after a moment, crawling out from under the cupboard and pushing the box I'd been using to the side. I brushed tendrils of dark, curly hair out of my face. My bun had gotten sloppy as the day wore on, and I knew even my dark brown skin couldn't hide the flush on my cheeks from the exertion of moving around.

Tracy Williams, the Hemlock Inn's general manager, strode over to my side and gripped under my arms, helping me into a standing position.

"Why are you on the ground? I thought you were taking it easy today."

"I am. We got this order of toiletries, and I wanted to get the box unpacked in case we need anything." I gestured to the box by the cupboard.

We usually kept all our toiletries in the back offices, but extra products ended up in this cupboard in the lobby. I didn't tell Tracy this, but we actually didn't need to use the overflow cupboard right now. The box had just been too heavy for me to carry into the office on my own.

"You're going to make this worse. Honestly, you shouldn't even be here right now." Tracy crossed her arms and narrowed her eyes, a silver nose ring poking out of her dark skin. She didn't let me get away with much, including working when my body was fighting against me.

Two days ago, I'd slipped on a puddle of rainwater in the lobby, landing on my back and seeing stars. I'd thought I was okay after that, but back pain had settled in overnight and gotten worse as the days went on. I didn't want to abandon the inn, though. As the owner of this place, it was my job to keep it running smoothly, and I wasn't going to let a little back pain stop me.

I waved my hand flippantly. "I'm fine, I'm fine. I'll take it easy, I promise. Besides, with Nadia off today, we need me here to cover her shift. Do you want me to abandon the inn?"

"No," Tracy said, "but we've got other people who can come in and take over while you rest up. That's what we pay them for, to be ready to take a shift. You're not thinking straight."

She might've been right about that, but again, I wasn't going to admit anything to her. The holidays had come and gone, and things were finally quiet at the Hemlock Inn.

Having a hurt back and needing to take the day off to rest would just disrupt the flow we'd created for ourselves here.

"I'm going to go check on the bistro," I said instead, moving out from behind the front desk.

Lola, the inn's resident beagle, lifted her head from her dog bed as I went past, but apparently, she didn't think it was worth following after me. I left Tracy and Lola at the front desk and went in search of a cup of tea.

I'd been the owner of the Hemlock Inn for about five months, and I was finally starting to get a handle on how things were run. I didn't want to let a little injury like this get in the way of running the inn.

Tracy had been around for about fifteen years, ever since my Aunt Sylvia hired her to help with running the day-to-day of the inn. When my Aunt Sylvia passed away late last year, she'd surprisingly left me the inn. Tracy and I had butted heads when I'd first shown up to town, but we had eventually found a good working relationship. I didn't want this back pain to get in the way.

Tracy was much more experienced at running the inn than I was, and I viewed us as partners, rather than business owner and employee. She had good insights into how to make this place successful, and I trusted what she had to say. Just not when it came to my back pain—I was the best judge of that.

Pushing open the door to the attached bistro, I was pleased to see it bustling with patrons—a mix of guests and townspeople. I nodded and waved to a few people I recognized from around town as I walked to the kitchen.

We'd had a busy holiday season, and Hank, the bistro's chef, had been working around the clock to make sure everyone was happy and well fed. I'd finally forced him to take some time off at the end of the year, as he was starting to forget orders and looked like he needed a break. He came back from two weeks in Hawaii with sunburned cheeks and red skin on the tips of his ears, which still hadn't faded after a week of being back in the Washington state clouds and rain. He was stirring something at the stove and glanced up when I came through the kitchen door.

"Ah, Simone, perfect timing!" He waved a spoon in my direction. "Can you help Javier with that?" He motioned to another man in the kitchen, who was carrying a stack of plates.

"I need to grab that towel from up there," Javier explained, gesturing to the top of a metal shelf with his chin. His white apron stood out against his brown skin, not a speck of food to be seen anywhere on the older man.

Javier was in charge of getting Hank's dishes onto plates and out to the servers out front in a timely manner. Though it was only the two of them back here, they ran like a well-oiled machine.

"Of course," I said, stepping up to the shelf. Javier was at least five inches taller than me, but I was always up for helping my employees.

I reached up for the towel, then let out a gasp as another burst of pain shot through my back. Hank put down his spoon and hurried to my side.

"See? You're in pain. You need to go home," he said, slipping his arm under mine and holding me up.

"Why would you make me reach for that?" I said, wincing from the pain. Were these people trying to kill me?

"We're just looking out for you," Hank said, his voice apologetic. "We figured if we could get you to reach for the towel, you'd see that you shouldn't be working right now."

"I'll be fine. I'll rest up tonight and come in early tomorrow. You don't need to worry about me."

"We didn't mean to make it worse, but we just wanted to show that you really should be resting," Javier said. "Whatever is wrong with your back, you don't want it to get worse."

I resisted the urge to tell him to mind his own beeswax. I had to remember that these people cared about me, even if it felt like they were smothering me.

"Javier's right," Hank said. "This isn't good for your back."

I tried not to roll my eyes. I came back here to see if they needed my help, not to get lectured at or tricked into making my back hurt more just to prove a point. "I'm perfectly fine. I'm going to leave now."

I sent them both a withering gaze and left the kitchen, hiding the groan that slipped out as I tried to stand up straight. I stood at the entrance to the bistro for a moment, watching everyone eating. Clearly, my back was telling me I needed to go home and rest. I sighed deeply, thinking about the bumpy car ride to my apartment in town.

"Oh, Simone, how nice to see you," Estelle called from her table, her gray hair pulled back into a low bun.

Estelle and Miles Adler had been my first friends when I'd come to Pine Brook. They'd also helped me with one or two murder investigations in the time I'd been here. They were retired but more active than most people my age.

We chatted for a few minutes, me trying unsuccessfully to cover up any signs of pain I was feeling from my back. Estelle narrowed her eyes at me, not likely to miss anything.

"Dear, you don't seem so well," she said.

I waved away her concerns, trying to hide my face. "I'm fine. I think I just slept funny. Nothing to worry about." They knew that I'd taken a fall, but they didn't need to know it was still hurting days later.

Estelle balled her hands into fists and stuck them on her

hips. "No fooling me, missy. You look like you're in more pain than a dog left out in the rain."

I didn't know what that meant, but I shook my head. "I'm fine, I swear. I just need to take things a little slower."

Such as no more getting tricked into reaching up to high shelves by my employees.

Miles leaned forward in his seat, concern written on his face. "You look like you should be lying down. If you don't rest, how will you ever get better?"

"I've got this great doctor in town," Estelle said. "Doctor Liam Bennett. He can take a look at your back and prescribe you something for the pain. Here, I'll write down his office number."

I shifted my weight between my feet while she scribbled something down on a scrap piece of paper she found on the table, wishing I hadn't come back here in the first place, but knowing I wouldn't get away without taking the number from her. She passed it to me, and I slipped it into my pocket, my heart warming at the sight of their faces. These people really did care for me. Maybe they were right, and I should go home and rest.

I thanked Estelle and Miles for their help and went back to the front desk. I'd see if I could get a bit more paperwork done, then I'd head home early. I'd do as much work as I could, as I felt bad about leaving the inn like this, but I couldn't help anyone if I was in as much pain as a dog left out in the rain. Whatever that meant.

"We don't need your help out here." Tracy smiled up at me from behind the front desk, stopping me before I had a chance to get to work. "Go. Home."

"Fine," I said, sticking my tongue out at her and turning back to the lobby. I would go home. Just as soon as I cleaned up a spill someone had left on the floor of the lobby. Can't have guests tripping in puddles, now, can we?

We had cleaners for this, but right now, it was about the principle of the thing. I grabbed a bucket of soapy water and a mop from the laundry room and went back to the lobby.

"Excuse me?" said a woman entering the lobby.

She was a couple inches taller than me, with light brown skin, luscious dark brown hair falling down the sides of her face in waves, and a dark mole on her right cheek. I guessed she was in her late thirties based on her piercing dark eyes, though her flawless skin and shiny hair gave her an ageless look. She was wearing a white suit with gold accents, immaculately tailored, with black Louboutin shoes—I spotted the red bottoms as she walked. Bracelets jingled on her wrists.

"I was hoping to speak with the owner," she said, her voice husky. A Spanish accent marked her words. "Do you know where I can find him?"

This wasn't the first time someone had assumed the owner of the Hemlock was a man, so I held back an eye roll. This woman didn't look like a guest, though. No bags in her hands, and guests didn't normally ask for the owner on arrival.

"I'm the owner," I said, taking a step closer to the woman.

Just then, my back spasmed again, and the bucket of soapy water I was holding jerked into the air. I watched, in horror and unable to move, as the water flew out of the bucket and landed all over this glamorous woman.

2

"I'm fine, I promise. This is all completely unnecessary," I insisted.

"You threw water on a guest! I don't think that counts as fine." Estelle's voice was firm. There was no arguing with her.

Tracy stood on the other side of me, staring down at me with her hands on her hips. She'd called in Eddy and Javier from the bistro to help the woman whose outfit I'd ruined, while she and Estelle had led me out to the courtyard to sit.

Nick Yoshida had strolled into the inn right while I was making a fool of myself in front of everyone, and he'd hurried over to help make sure I was okay. I wasn't thrilled about any of them seeing me in pain like this, especially not the cute produce guy I'd been flirting with for the past few months.

"You need to go see a doctor," Tracy said, her tone serious. "This back injury has gotten out of hand."

"It's not that big of a deal. Nadia's still gone, and I'm sure you need help at the front desk. I can still work, see?" I attempted to stand to prove my point but cried out in pain as my back protested against the movement. Maybe she was right about seeing a doctor...

Tracy crossed her arms sternly, not letting me get away with anything. "You don't need to worry about that at all. We've spent all week trying to get you to rest your back, and now that you've made a mess all over a guest, we're not going to let you avoid the doctor anymore. Penny and Eddy will help out at the front desk if needed. Remember, I ran this place for several months on my own before you showed up. I can handle it."

"Fine," I relented. I hated the thought of being away from the inn, as it felt like the one place where my presence truly mattered, but trying to work with a messed up back would only make things worse. I cringed as I remembered the look on that guest's face when she realized I'd ruined her shoes.

"Okay, you're right. I'll go see a doctor. I'm guessing that Dr. Bennett guy is my best option?"

"Yes!" Estelle began hopping on the balls of her feet. "He's one of the best in town, and he's always got availability in the middle of the day. His clinic is right off downtown."

"Didn't they find that poor girl who'd overdosed in the river that runs behind the clinic?" I asked, remembering the story that had been all over the newspaper last week. It was one of the first deaths in Pine Brook that I'd seen that hadn't been murder.

"Yes, that was really tragic," Tracy said with a shiver. "I get the jeebies just driving past that creek now."

Tracy never seemed to get flustered by all the death in this town, but an overdose was especially sad.

"Dr. Bennett mentioned they had to close for a day while the police investigated behind the clinic, but he said they haven't had any issues since then. I should warn you, though," Estelle added. "He's got a nurse who can be a bit prickly."

I grimaced at the thought. "Are you sure this is the best doctor for me to see? I'm not really in the mood for prickly nurses."

"Trust me, you're going to love my doctor. He's a very sweet man and not too bad on the eyes, if you know what I mean," she added with a wink and a nudge. Tracy snorted, and Nick hid a smile behind his hand.

"Estelle!" I said with a laugh. "Isn't your husband nearby?"

Estelle waved her hand flippantly. "I meant for you, of course. Miles and I are perfectly happy, thank you very much," she added with a sniff.

I rolled my eyes. I wasn't interested in dating a doctor, although three months ago, I might've felt differently. These days, flirting with a certain produce farmer was keeping me very distracted. My cheeks warmed as I made eye contact with Nick.

"Still, he's a very good doctor," Estelle went on. "I take these soy supplements, which I could get online, but he wanted to make sure I was getting reputable pills, so he always puts in a prescription for me."

"Why do you take soy supplements?"

She shrugged. "Years ago, my doctor told me I should start taking them when I was having hot flashes during menopause."

I paused, waiting for her to say more and answer the question that had immediately popped into my head, but she didn't say anything else.

"You still have hot flashes?" I finally asked. Estelle was at least seventy, which didn't make any sense. "I didn't realize hot flashes lasted so long." Was this what I had to look forward to come menopause?

Estelle winked. "It keeps my bones strong."

I wasn't a doctor; maybe they did help with her bones. Whatever made her happy.

"All right, now that we know what pills Estelle takes, I think it's time we get you to that health clinic," Tracy said, her voice louder than necessary as she tried to take back control of the conversation. "I'm guessing you're in no condition to drive yourself, and I should probably stay here to keep an eye on things."

"I can take her," Nick piped up. A smile spread across his face as he looked down at me. "I stopped by to check on that last order of veggies I dropped off for Hank, but I'm not in a hurry to get back to the farm just yet."

"Excellent," Tracy said. "Let's get you into his truck."

I didn't have a chance to protest as the three of them pulled me up from the outdoor couch and led me back into the inn. It wasn't like I didn't like spending time with Nick, far from it, but I still sometimes got a little tongue-tied whenever I was around him. Still, I needed to see a doctor, and he was my only transportation option at this point.

The three of them led me out the back door of the inn. Fortunately, I didn't have to see any concerned faces in the lobby. I was still mortified about what I had done and wanted to put some distance between myself and the glamorous guest whose clothes I'd ruined.

Outside, the sky was gray and the wind had picked up since that morning. Tracy had run off and grabbed my coat from the lobby, so at least I was warm, but all I really wanted to do was snuggle up in front of the fire. Instead, I let the three of them help me up into Nick's truck, trying not to wince as my back protested the movements. Nick climbed into the cab with me and pulled away from the inn. Tracy and Estelle stood at the back door, watching us leave.

"Thanks for giving me a ride," I said after a few moments of silence. "I probably have been pushing myself too hard with this back pain and should've gone home to rest sooner."

"Yeah, well, I understand that desire to keep working, even when you're not feeling well," Nick said with a shrug. "I get that way at the farm. It's especially hard when you don't have someone who can easily take over for you. You're lucky to have Tracy to help run the inn."

I nodded. He was right. Tracy and I made things so much easier for each other. We were lucky to have the other around. Nick's father used to run his farm, but he'd been sick for a while, and Nick had to do most of the work himself now.

The road leading from the inn into town was surrounded by forest, the branches of the trees mostly bare in the winter. Tension eased out of my back at the slight rocking of the car as we drove.

"How's the farm?" I asked after a few moments of comfortable silence. Why had I been so nervous about being alone with Nick? He had a way of making all the stress melt away by his presence.

"The farm is fine. Winter is always a weird season for us. I spend most of my time making sure the crops can make it to the spring. But we get some good winter veggies this time of year, too. I dropped off a box of broccoli and kale at the inn yesterday, and Hank was pretty excited to see it."

As he changed gears and shifted in his seat, a small item fell out of the pocket of his hoodie. I grabbed it before it had a chance to fall to the floor.

"What's this?" I asked, holding the small, rectangular

item. The leather encasing it was worn, with imprints from hands. This was a well-used item, whatever it was.

"It's a Higonokami knife," he said, reaching over and pressing his thumb against the item. Suddenly, a blade, about three inches long, popped out.

"Whoa!" I dropped the knife into my lap. "Why would you hand me a weapon?"

He laughed and gently took it back from me, flicking the blade back into place and slipping it back into his pocket, his attention never once leaving the road. "I didn't think you'd hurt yourself."

"Why do you have that thing? Are you planning on robbing a bank later?"

"It was my grandfather's. He brought it with him to the States when he left Japan. He gave it to my dad, who gave it to me a few years ago. It needs a cleaning, so I was planning on dropping it off at this specialty shop in Holliston later today."

I cocked my head to the side. "Have you killed anyone with it?"

His laugh was sudden and loud, filling the car. "No, I have not committed murder with it, though I shouldn't be surprised you'd ask that. Isn't your whole thing, finding killers?" he added with a wink.

I smirked. "I just call it like I see it."

He laughed and pulled the knife back out, flicking open the blade, then snapping it shut, over and over, like a nervous tic.

"I don't even think my grandpa did anything nefarious with it. He claims he needed to protect himself back when he was in Japan, but I think he just thought it was cool. He did tell me once that it gave him good luck, so I like to keep it around for that reason."

"Well, I hope it brings you good luck soon." I smiled, content to sit in this car with him for the rest of the day.

Every time we were together, I felt more and more comfortable with Nick, and it was nice to be with someone who was so open and honest. I'd had my fair share of cheating boyfriends in the past, and it was a pleasant change to be with someone who didn't have to hide anything. I opened my mouth again, ready to take the leap and finally ask him out on a date, when Nick spoke.

"Here we are," he said, coming to a stop in the clinic's parking lot. "Ready to head inside?"

Drat. Guess it wasn't the best time to ask him out. I should probably focus on healing my back before making any moves on my crush.

"Ready as I'll ever be." I pulled off my seat belt and began to slowly exit the car, taking care not to aggravate my back.

Nick helped me down from his truck, and we slowly made our way into the waiting room of Pine Brook Family Physicians, which was located just off downtown Pine Brook.

I checked in with the receptionist, a woman named Maria with a big smile and even bigger dark hair.

"Take a seat and the doctor will be with you shortly," Maria said, gesturing to the waiting room behind us.

Her voice was breathy, with her Puerto Rican accent shimmering under the surface. I pegged her to be in her sixties. The framed photos scattered around her desk were evidence of her large family.

Nick pulled his cell phone out of his pocket and began scrolling through his emails as we settled into our seats, while I looked around the rest of the waiting room. The large room had comfortable chairs and small tables scattered about, with dozens of magazines for people to read. A TV whirred in the corner of the ceiling, turned to some morning talk show, the volume low, but no one was watching. Brightly colored toys were strewn around in the corner —Legos, trucks, and stuffed animals—and several children sat on the ground playing with them.

The large second-story windows looked out onto Pine Brook and let in a ton of light. The waiting room was about half full. There was a mix of ages, from a young teen cradling her pregnant belly to a towering gentleman who looked older than Estelle, folding and refolding a white handkerchief. Several parents kept glancing over and checking on their kids in the play area, and everyone looked tired. I guess you didn't show up to the doctor's office if you were feeling good.

"Simone Evans." A nurse had come out of the back area into the waiting room, holding a clipboard and looking around the room.

Nick reached over and squeezed my hand. "I'll be here when you get back," he said, nodding towards the woman who'd said my name.

I sent him a tiny smile and stood, clutching my purse and jacket and walking over to the nurse, who wore maroon scrubs and had her hair pulled back tightly into a bun.

It wasn't as if I was afraid of going to see the doctor; of course not, that would've been silly. I just really hoped they wouldn't prod me with anything sharp.

The nurse led me back through a set of doors to the rest of the doctor's office. Past the waiting room, this part of the office was more sterile, with medical equipment beeping in the corners and bins for waste scattered throughout the hallway. But someone had still tried to make it homey, painting the walls a bright yellow and hanging impressionist and abstract paintings on the walls. Doors led off from either side of us, presumably to examining rooms and offices. The nurse kept up a fast pace, and I had to stop staring all around me to keep up with her. My back fiercely protested the pace, but she barely seemed to notice my struggles.

A woman who I assumed was a doctor, given her white lab coat, stepped out from one of the offices, clutching a folder in one hand. She glanced up when she heard us approach, her eyes passing over me and landing on the nurse.

"Oh, Gayle, do you have those test results?" she asked, holding her arm out to catch the nurse's attention and stop her from walking further down the hallway.

The nurse, Gayle, paused and looked up at the doctor. She was a beautiful woman, tall, with striking features and long dark hair flowing loose down her back. I thought she might be Chinese-American, but only because she looked so much like Lucy Liu. I'd loved the film version of *Charlie's Angels* as a kid, watching the movie every week with my sister and pretending to be spies.

"I emailed them to you this morning. Do you need me to print you out a copy, too, Doctor?" Gayle replied.

My head shot up at her tone. I hadn't spent much time around doctors and nurses, but the way she asked about printing out the results indicated that she thought the doctor was an idiot for needing the results printed.

The doctor's eyes narrowed for the briefest of seconds, then her features smoothed out, and she smiled at Gayle, though the smile didn't reach her eyes.

"Thank you," she said to Gayle. "No need to print."

Her eyes glided over me, giving me a slight nod, before continuing on. I turned and watched her walk through another door in the hallway, her head held high and her heels—which were designer, as far as I could tell—clacking against the hallway floor.

Clearly, I'd stumbled onto some tension between the employees at this clinic. This must be the prickly nurse Estelle had mentioned. All I cared about was getting some relief for my back and getting out of here. Whatever drama was occurring between this nurse and doctor was none of my business.

"This way." Gayle's raised voice startled me.

I spun around, finding her standing at the door to one of the rooms, so I hurried over, my head down and my cheeks warming at being caught spying on someone.

Gayle held open the door to the examining room, and I slid past her, entering the small space. It looked like every other examining room I'd ever been in. The lighting was harsh, though more muted than the bulbs from outside in the hallway.

The room contained an exam bed with a paper sheet covering it, a large computer on a stand with a wheeled stool in front, cabinets, drawers along all of the walls, and posters and pamphlets for every ailment scattered on every surface. I stepped into the room and put my bag on the single chair in the corner for guests, and turned back to Gayle.

She took me through all the standard things you do when you first show up to the doctor. She took my temperature, the ear thermometer cold as she shoved it in, and had me stand on a scale to take my weight. I glanced away from the display as the numbers flashed—no need to spend the rest of the day with some number dancing through my head. Then she had me stand against the wall near a chart to measure my height, and took my blood pressure.

She was silent the entire time she worked, moving efficiently but keeping her head down. This gave me a moment to study her. She was in her fifties, a bit younger than the woman at the front desk, but Gayle was much taller than Maria. Her shoulders were wide, her chest broad. Her scrubs looked worn, though clean, and her sneakers practically blinded me with their whiteness as they squeaked along the floor.

Her light-colored hair was somewhere between blonde and gray. The lines etched into her face gave it a stern look, indicating that the lines didn't come from much smiling or laughing over the years.

"What are you here for?" Gayle asked.

"I've been experiencing some back pain. I think I pulled a muscle or something a few days ago, and it's getting worse," I said. "My friend Estelle suggested I come here to get it checked."

Gayle typed at the computer while I talked, presumably taking notes for the doctor, but her fingers slowed when I said Estelle's name. She glanced up at me, her brow furrowed and suspicious.

"Estelle Adler?" she asked. "You're friends with Estelle?"

I nodded. Why had she stopped typing?

"Yes. I'm new in town, only been here for a few months, and Estelle said her doctor was great."

"You shouldn't trust everything Estelle says," Gayle said, focusing back on the computer. "She's been known to have poor judgment before."

I opened my mouth to respond, then snapped it shut. Why was she saying this to me? Did Gayle and Estelle have some history I wasn't aware of? Why hadn't Estelle mentioned any of this to me? What kind of history had I stumbled onto at this clinic?

3

A tap came at the door, opening to reveal a man in a white lab coat. Gayle's face brightened at his entrance. I did a double take at her wide smile, as I hadn't realized she could look that happy about anything. Glancing back at the man, I could understand why.

He was tall, most likely in his forties, with flowing blond hair pushed back from his forehead and a solid frame. His green eyes crinkled, and I had a feeling the lines on his face did, in fact, come from smiling. His movie-star good looks were surprising in this drab office, though I could now understand why Estelle kept coming back here, even if she did have a bad history with Gayle.

"Hello, ladies, how are we doing today?" he asked, looking between Gayle and me.

"We were just finishing up," Gayle said, typing a few things into her notes and smiling up at the doctor. "My notes should be entered into the system now."

Her smile dropped when she looked back at me, and then she was out of the room, the door shutting softly behind her.

"I'm Liam Bennett." The doctor turned to me and held out his hand. I slipped my hand into his, getting a chill at how tiny my hand felt in his.

"Simone Evans," I replied, shaking his hand. "Thanks for seeing me on such short notice. Estelle Adler speaks very highly of you."

"Well, I'm glad." Dr. Bennett smiled and looked down at his folder bashfully. He took a seat on the stool by the computer. "Estelle's a great woman. She's been coming here for years. I'm glad to hear she still thinks we're worth showing up for."

"I think she just got tired of me complaining about my back pain," I said with a shrug, and the doctor laughed.

After meeting Gayle, even given Estelle's glowing endorsement of him, I'd expected the doctor to be cold and unfeeling, but this man was personable and engaging. Why would he hire someone so grumpy?

"Not that it's any of my business," I said. "But is your nurse having a bad day? She was a little...grumpy with me."

Dr. Bennett quirked his mouth, acknowledging that he knew exactly what I was talking about. "She can be a little abrasive at first. We're a small team here, and Gayle is our main nurse, so she's usually pretty swamped and needs to keep things moving. Dr. Li and I—that's the other doctor here—have been talking about bringing on some additional help for Gayle, but we can't quite justify it in the budget."

I didn't mention anything about what Gayle had said about Estelle. If this man thought Gayle was so good at her job, I didn't want to go around bad-mouthing her when I didn't have the full story. Maybe we had just gotten off on the wrong foot. I didn't really know what her history was with Estelle, but that didn't have to influence our relationship, as superficial as it was.

"Now"—he put his folder onto the desk and turned to me fully in the stool—"what seems to be the issue?"

"I slipped a few days ago, and my back has been in pain ever since. I've been trying to work through it, and didn't think much of the pain at first. But then earlier today, I had a little...mishap." I shifted in my seat at the embarrassing memory, causing a small ripple of pain to shoot down my back, making me wince.

Dr. Bennett paused in his note taking and raised his eyebrows, as if waiting for me to elaborate on the mishap. He didn't need to know about the gorgeous white suit I no doubt ruined, so I moved on quickly.

"My friends convinced me to come in, and I want to make sure it's not anything more serious," I went on, skipping over any elaboration of my mishap.

He typed a few notes into the computer, then stood and began his examination. He slipped off his stethoscope and gestured to me.

"Mind if I take a listen?" he asked, and I scooted forward to give him access to my torso.

He slipped the stethoscope down the back of my shirt, and we stood for a few moments in silence while I took some breaths.

Next, he felt along my back, pressing lightly into some areas of the skin. I winced a few times as he got too close to the more sensitive parts. He noted a few areas with bruises that I couldn't see and had me do some stretches to indicate what my range of motion was.

"Well, it does seem like you've pulled something and simply need to rest it," he said once he was done. He sat on the stool and wrote a few additional notes. "I don't think it warrants x-rays at this point, but I agree with the assessment that what you need now is rest. It's a good thing you came here when you did, as more time on your feet could've made this much worse." He pulled a pad of paper out of one of the drawers and picked up a pen.

"I'm going to write you a prescription for pain medication and muscle relaxers, which you can get filled in town, and you should alternate heat and ice on your back until it starts to feel better. You can come back in a couple of days if you haven't improved." He ripped off the piece of paper he'd been scribbling on and passed it to me. I studied the words on the paper, wondering how the pharmacist would possibly read the scribbles.

"Now, I should warn you," he went on, his tone serious. "These pain pills can be addictive. You should only take as much as the prescription suggests, and you should try to avoid taking any of the pills if you can. The first couple of days will probably be the worst in terms of your pain, but I want you to listen to your body and stop taking them when you feel like you don't need them any longer. Estelle will know where to go to get that prescription filled. Any questions?"

I shook my head, slipping the prescription into my pocket. He hadn't told me anything I didn't already know, but hopefully this medication would help with the pain.

"Thank you so much," I said, slowly standing up. "I'll let you know if anything changes."

"Of course," he said with a smile. "You should be good in no time."

Dr. Bennett stepped out of the examining room to give me a moment to collect my things, then walked me down the hallway back to the waiting room. He held the door open for me.

"Don't forget to fill that prescription," he said, nodding to my pocket.

"I promise," I said with a smile.

He sent me a wink, then stepped back into the hallway and shut the door behind him.

Back in the waiting room, Nick was still sitting in his seat, scrolling through his phone. There were fewer people in the waiting room than there had been before. As I walked over in his direction, someone started yelling at the front of the waiting room.

All the heads in the waiting room swiveled over to the front desk. Maria sat behind it, getting yelled at and looking petrified.

"How many times do I have to tell you?" Gayle yelled from behind the desk. "The pipettes need to go with the syringes, not the gauze. Are you always this much of an idiot?" She shook a box at Maria, gauze shaking around inside.

Maria's eyes glanced around the waiting room like a wounded animal as everyone watched this interaction.

"Maybe we should talk about this in the back?" she said to Gayle, her voice squeaking out so quietly, we all had to lean in to hear her better.

"No, you just need to learn how to do your job," Gayle said, dumping the box on Maria's desk.

She rolled her eyes and stormed past me back through the door I'd just come through, barely glancing at me or anyone else in the waiting room. The door slammed behind her, and no one said anything.

What was that all about? Hadn't Dr. Bennett just said Gayle wasn't so bad once you got to know her? After what I'd just seen, I'd be surprised if someone wasn't plotting her death as we spoke.

4

The waiting room was quiet after Gayle's departure. No one in the room moved, and everyone looked unsure about what to do. We couldn't all stand here forever, so I walked over to Maria.

"Are you all right?" I asked her.

Her head hung low, her arms wrapped around herself, as if she was trying to sink into the ground. Her head snapped up at my words.

"Y-yes," she said, her voice shaky. "Gayle can be so dramatic sometimes," she added with a laugh, though she couldn't hide the distress in her voice.

"Should I get one of the doctors and tell them what happened?"

"No!" Maria said, her voice much louder than it had been, causing me to jump. My eyebrows shot up my face at her outburst.

"Sorry." She chuckled, though there wasn't any joy in her voice. "I don't want to bother the doctors. It's no big deal. Gayle's just had a busy day."

"That doesn't give her the right to speak to you that way," I said.

Maria's cheeks turned pink. "I think it's best if we leave it alone. Did you need anything else?" she asked me, her voice turning business-like. "A follow-up appointment or anything?"

I shook my head, still feeling like Gayle shouldn't be allowed to get away with yelling at people, but not wanting to force Maria to do something she didn't want to do.

"No, I got a prescription. Thanks for all of your help."

Dr. Bennett leaned over the counter behind reception, causing the receptionist to jump in surprise at his sudden appearance. "Maria, did you hear back from the alarm company?"

She shook her head, trying to hide how upset she was. "They might be able to come in a week."

He frowned. "I really wish they would get out here quickly." He leaned in closer to Maria and dropped his voice, though he didn't seem to notice that Nick and I were within hearing distance. "We can't go on with a broken alarm system for much longer," he murmured to her, flipping through some patient files she'd had stacked on her desk.

"I'll call them again." She sniffed and wiped at her nose with a tissue.

Dr. Bennett patted her shoulder and walked back down the hallway, his head buried in the patient file he'd picked up. He didn't seem to notice that his receptionist was having a breakdown, or that the entire waiting room was completely silent after Gayle's outburst.

"Well, we should get going," Nick said after a few moments of tense silence.

I shot Maria a consoling smile, then followed Nick out of

the health clinic. We were quiet as we left the building. The sun had started to peek its head out of the clouds while we were inside, but the air was still chilly. Nick and I hurried to his truck and climbed in, blasting the heater once we were safely locked inside.

"That was pretty intense," I said as he pulled out of the parking lot. "Is Gayle normally like that?"

"I've never seen an outburst like that before, but I think Estelle was right about her being prickly. I hope Maria is going to be okay."

I murmured my agreement, staring out the window as the streets rolled by. Gayle's mention of not trusting Estelle had seemed strange at the time, but maybe Gayle was just the kind of person to have bad relationships with many people. Still, I'd expect a nurse to be kind and gentle and, while Gayle had done a good job of examining me and hadn't treated me poorly, her interactions with others at the clinic left something to be desired.

"Did you get a prescription?" Nick asked, interrupting my thoughts.

I nodded, pulling out the slip of paper. "Is there a pharmacy we can go to?"

"There sure is," Nick said, switching on his blinker and checking his rearview mirror.

I pushed all thoughts of Estelle and Gayle out of my head, ready to spend my time resting and healing. Their dramatic past was none of my concern right now.

THREE DAYS LATER, I stood in line at Cuppa Joe's, reading the menu written on the chalkboard behind the front counter, trying to decide if I wanted a scone to go with my coffee. It was early, not yet eight A.M., and I didn't want to show up at the inn with a scone from Cuppa Joe's and make Hank think I didn't like his cooking. By the time I got to the front counter, I put in an order for a single coffee, promising myself I'd pick up whatever pastry Hank had available in the bistro once he served breakfast.

Cuppa Joe's was quiet this morning. People sat at the scattered tables, reading books or typing away at computers, most with coffee, some with scones. The floor-to-ceiling windows around the front door let in the sun, and I looked out the windows as I waited for my coffee. I was surprised that so many people were here this early, but clearly there was a contingent of early-morning coffee drinkers in Pine Brook.

After a couple days of rest and liberal use of the pain pills, I'd woken up feeling great. I finally felt ready to get out of my apartment and go back into the world. I wanted to check on things at the inn, but needed some coffee to get my day going.

The bell over the door tinkled as it was pushed open, and Nick strode through. He was wearing dark pants and a button-down with a dark jacket and a belt. A far cry from the jeans and t-shirts he normally wore. He got in line and put in his order, and I waved when he left the counter to wait for his drink. He smiled and crossed the room to come stand by me.

"You're here early," he said by way of greeting. "I like to get here before the crowds show up, but I don't think I've seen you here this early before."

"I know, it is early for me. I slept so much these past couple of days that I woke up really early this morning and wanted to get an early start at the inn."

"How are you feeling? You look much better today."

"Thanks," I said with a smile, dropping my gaze down. "I am feeling much better. Finally have the energy to go into the inn today. But I couldn't go without picking up some coffee first."

"I know how you feel," he said, running his hand through his dark hair. "I've got a meeting at the bank today about the farm, and this was my first stop."

"Everything okay with the farm?"

Nick nodded. "Just the monthly meeting I have with the bank to make sure our finances are all in order. They like when you make an effort," he added, gesturing down to his clothes, and I nodded as realization dawned. Of course— Nick wasn't likely to put on a shirt with buttons unless he absolutely needed to.

"We did have something pretty wild happen at the farm recently," Nick added. "A possum got stuck in the rafters of the barn, and we had to call the vet to help get her down. The vet didn't know what to do with a stuck possum, so then I had to call the fire department, and they spent about twenty minutes standing around debating whether it was considered animal abuse to forcibly remove the possum from the rafters. I told them it was animal abuse to keep the poor thing up in the rafters like that, but they were pretty uncomfortable about it." He laughed, shaking his head, his eyes crinkling. "I'm still not quite sure what part of me thought it was a good idea to take over running the farm, but here we are."

I smiled, feeling myself leaning closer to Nick as he spoke. I'd spent the past few days stuck in bed and in pain, and it felt good to finally get back out into the world. Plus, I could listen to Nick talk about his farm all day. The twinkle in his eyes as he discussed the antics of the animals always sent a chill down my spine.

I took a deep breath, the words tumbling out of me before I could stop them. "Hey, I've heard Cheesy Does It has a new 'mountain of cheese' special. Want to go check it out with me?"

Nick's face brightened, but before he could respond, my name was called out at the front counter as a barista stepped forward with my coffee. I twisted around to see what was happening, which sent my back into a spasm of pain that had me gasping. I guess I wasn't as recovered as I'd initially thought!

"Simone, are you okay?" Nick reached out to steady me as I groaned, but I shook my head, not wanting him to touch me, only focused on digging out one of the pills Dr. Bennett had prescribed me. I'd woken up feeling great and hadn't taken one of the pills, but it was clear I needed it now, and the idea of anyone touching me while spasms coursed down my back was too much to handle.

"I'll grab your coffee," Nick said quickly, once he realized I was focused on getting some pain relief.

The pill bottle had a cap on it that would stump a magician, and I tried not to groan in pain as I struggled with the cap. What kind of monster would design something so hard to open?

"Here you go, Simone." Nick's voice came from behind me, jolting me out of my intense focus on the pill bottle. Fortunately, I managed to unscrew the cap at the last moment, but unfortunately, my jolt caused me to fling the bottle into the air, pills scattering around the coffee shop.

One pill remained in the bottle. I groaned, pouring it out into my hand and tossing it into my mouth, grabbing the coffee from Nick and taking a swallow to wash down the pill. I grimaced as the hot coffee coursed down my throat. I hadn't even had a chance to add a little milk and sugar first!

"Sorry about that," Nick said, his cheeks pink from embarrassment. He held his coffee cup in his other hand. "Are you okay?"

I nodded, already feeling the spasm in my back begin to loosen. "I'm fine. Although now I need to go back to the clinic to get another prescription written." Someone had come out of the back of the coffee shop and started sweeping up my ruined pills. I wasn't getting those back any time soon, and Dr. Bennett hadn't put any refills on the prescription he'd given me initially.

A crash sounded from the front of the coffee shop, and everyone looked up at the noise. Gayle was standing at the counter, her hands on her hips. I couldn't hold back a groan. Oh no, what was she upset about now?

Nick and I took a couple of steps closer to the counter, as if we were expecting Gayle to have a fit, and we'd need to restrain her. She'd slammed down a coffee cup, sloshing some of the coffee onto the counter. She was the only person standing in line, but all the patrons in the coffee shop had turned their attention to her outburst at the counter. The woman behind the counter, Stella, I think her name was, had a wary, guarded expression on her face.

"I come in every day. You should know my order by now," Gayle said, her voice raised.

"This is your order." Stella held out the coffee cup. "Black coffee, two sugars, a splash of whole milk. Like you said, you come in every day. We aren't likely to get it wrong."

"Well, someone must've done something wrong because this is not what I normally order," Gayle said with a sniff.

"I don't know what to tell you. If you don't like the order, you can leave."

"I demand to speak with your manager!" Gayle shouted, her face tightening.

Stella sighed and visibly collapsed into herself a bit. "I am the manager. You know this already. Now, do you want the coffee or not?"

Gayle pulled the coffee up to her face and took a sniff, then grimaced. "This smells weird. You know I have a soy allergy. How do I know someone didn't slip in soy milk instead of regular milk just to mess with me?"

"We don't even put soy in our coffee!" Stella threw her hands up, exasperated. "No one in this town actually likes soy milk."

I had to agree with the townspeople there; soy milk tasted like watered-down milk that had been left out in the sun.

"Not yet, you don't. But how do I know you won't start putting it in the coffee someday, hmm?"

"Look, Gayle, there's no soy in your coffee, and you'll be the first to know once we start stocking it. Is there anything else I can get you, or are you going to leave now?" Stella looked about ready to throw the woman out herself, but she kept her mouth shut as she waited for an answer.

Gayle narrowed her eyes like she was going to say something else, gave a *harumph* instead, picked up her coffee cup, and turned and stormed out of the coffee shop. She swung her purse onto her shoulder, the Prada label flashing out across the room like a beacon. I wouldn't have guessed that this grumpy nurse, with her sensible shoes and severe bun, would have such an expensive bag.

She attempted to slam the door to the coffee shop behind her, but because of the way the door mechanism was set up, it simply slowed down and shut with a click, making for a much less dramatic exit.

The coffee shop was silent after she left. Gayle was much too loud for this early in the morning. Through the plate-glass window of the coffee shop, Gayle could be seen climbing into a tan Honda Civic and driving away.

I slipped the empty pill bottle I'd been struggling with back into my purse, then walked up to the front counter and grabbed a packet of sugar out of one of the little bins in the front. Stella wiped down the counter as I stirred the sugar into my coffee.

"Gayle seems like quite a handful," I said to Stella, adding a drop of creamer to my coffee and replacing the lid.

Stella rolled her eyes. "You're telling me. Half the time, she comes in and demands a drink that isn't on the menu, then the other half, she complains about the drink she always orders. You'd think, if she hated us so much, that she'd just go to a different coffee shop. We're not the only ones in Pine Brook. And yet, every day, she shows up with a new complaint. I think it's because we're so close to the doctor's office. She's not willing to walk an extra two blocks."

"Don't you have the right to refuse service to anyone?" I took a sip of my coffee, sighing as the caffeine made its way through my veins.

Stella shrugged and started wiping down the counter where Gayle had sloshed her coffee. "I could, but the owner doesn't really buy that saying. He'd rather we serve everyone we can to get the most profits. One of these days, Gayle is going to do something that hurts someone, and that person is going to sue the owner. Until then, I just keep my head down and do my best to help her."

What kind of business owner would knowingly put his employees in danger of Gayle's outbursts every single day? Once again, I was grateful I'd left working for someone else and accepted ownership of the Hemlock Inn. No business was worth the kind of hassle Gayle seemed to bring with her wherever she went.

"Well, thanks for the coffee," I said to Stella, holding the cup up in her direction. She nodded her acknowledgment and turned to the next customer in line.

I went back to Nick and by silent agreement, we left the coffee shop with our drinks. Fortunately, Gayle was nowhere to be seen outside.

"That was pretty intense," Nick said, turning to me and taking a sip of his coffee.

I nodded my agreement. "That was just as bad as when she yelled at Maria at the clinic. Why don't people tell her to cut it out?"

Nick shrugged. "I guess everyone's accepted that's who she is. She gives me my flu shot every year, and she's not exactly a ray of sunshine. Most people try to stay away from her. I'm surprised Stella keeps serving her, though. You'd think the owner would do something about it."

"Well, not all business owners can be as considerate as you." I smiled, pleased to see Nick's cheeks turn pink at the compliment. What else might I be able to say to get his cheeks to turn that adorable color?

"Do you want a ride to the clinic?" he asked. "I'm sure you'll need a new prescription written soon."

"No, thanks, I'm all right. The clinic doesn't open until nine, and I'd like to check on how things are going at the inn."

"Well, let me know if you need anything else. Oh, and I'd love to grab dinner with you at Cheesy Does It. I'll call you once I can look at my schedule to nail down a day. It's a date." He sent me a wink, then made his way to his car parked up the street.

I nearly swooned at the sight of that wink, glad to see that my embarrassing tussle in the coffee shop hadn't turned him off the idea of going out with me. We were going on a date! I couldn't wait to tell Estelle all about it.

I strolled over to my car and got behind the wheel, pondering the temper tantrum I'd witnessed at the coffee shop. If anyone should be embarrassed about what had happened in the coffee shop just now, it was Gayle. She really was quite a pain, and I was surprised to see that people didn't stand up to her generally. No one thought to question her rude and aggressive behavior?

I turned on the engine, pulled away from the curb and headed toward the inn. One day, someone was going to snap and tell Gayle how they really felt about her. I did not want to be around to see that volcano erupt.

5

Pulling up to the inn's parking lot, I switched off the engine and looked out the front windshield at the looming building. It was built in the Tudor style, with dark wood, a sloped roof, and various arches defining the style. Greenery climbed the walls, and I was looking forward to the spring, when all the flowers would bloom.

Twinkle lights shone from the arches, even during the day—we'd put them up in December and hadn't had the heart to take them down yet. They lent some nice atmosphere to the inn, at a time of year when normally things were gloomy and rainy.

Entering the inn, I was warmed by the crackling fire in the fireplace on the opposite wall. The lobby was quiet, the front desk empty, though I could hear murmurings and footsteps coming from further back in the inn. Lola, the beagle, poked her head around the side of the front desk and gave me a little bark. I went over to her and scratched her ears, taking up my post behind the front desk.

It felt good to be back. Lola seemed to miss me, and it was the first time in days that I'd actually put clothes on and gone out into the world. While witnessing Gayle's outburst at Cuppa Joe's had put a damper on my morning, being at the inn was already calming me down.

Tracy came through the door to the bistro and waved when she saw me at the front desk. Her black dreadlocks were piled on top of her head today, and her nose ring sparkled against her dark skin. She was carrying a stack of folders and passed them to me to start organizing once she got to the desk.

"You look much better today," she said, giving Lola's ears a scratch.

"I'm feeling a bit better, although I managed to tweak my back at Cuppa Joe's this morning. I'm going to need to go back to the clinic when it opens to get a new prescription written up." I opened one of the folders she'd handed me and glanced through the figures inside. "Hey, listen, what do you know about Gayle, the nurse at the clinic?"

"Gayle? Not much." Tracy pursed her lips, thinking. "I think she and her son live in town. I know she's a pain, but fortunately, I never get sick, so I don't have to see her much."

"You never get sick? What are you, some kind of super-hero? Don't worry, your secret identity is safe with me."

Tracy rolled her eyes and chuckled, straightening up the pile of folders she'd made on the counter.

"I saw Gayle at Cuppa Joe's this morning," I went on, "and she was yelling at poor Stella for something she didn't do. I get the sense she's always like that?"

Tracy shrugged. "Pretty much. Like I said, I try to stay away from her. I do know she's a huge gossip. You don't want her to know anything about you, because the second she does, it's all over town."

Was that all that Gayle was doing when she made vague references to Estelle, just trying to stir the pot? If she and

Estelle had some kind of dark history, Gayle might've wanted to do whatever she could to badmouth Estelle around town. Of course, she hadn't actually said anything negative about Estelle, but gossipmongers loved creating drama, right?

It was still strange that no one said anything to Gayle about how she treated people, especially given that Dr. Bennett didn't question her behavior with patients, but I wasn't going to get involved. I had other things to worry about.

"How are things here?" I asked Tracy. "Any issues while I was gone?"

"Nothing to worry about," Tracy said with a shrug. "January is always a little quieter, especially after the rush of the holidays, but nothing we can't handle."

She was right about the holidays. I'd been surprised at how booked up we were in December, though after I thought about it, it hadn't been that surprising. People were traveling and visiting family, and the Hemlock Inn was a great place to stay. I'd shown up to work one day in early December and stumbled onto crowds packed into the lobby, waiting to check in. Nadia and Tracy had handled it like pros, while I'd wandered around, gaping at everyone like a confused fish. I was going to make sure I remembered this next year, so I wasn't overwhelmed by all the people again.

"Listen, there was one thing I wanted to talk to you about," Tracy said, turning to me. "There's someone coming by to look at the inn tomorrow. I'm hoping you'll feel well enough to meet her. She wants to talk about the inn's financial future. Does tomorrow work for you?"

Wait, what? Someone wanted to talk about the future of our inn? Did Tracy want to make big changes to how we were running things here? Was she trying to sell the inn to someone? "What are you talking about?" I asked, only able to voice one question out of the million that were currently running through my head.

Before she had a chance to respond, Hank burst out of the bistro doors, covered in flour. "Uhh, can one of you help me back here?" he asked. "We had an issue with the ceiling fan and, um, some flour."

Tracy glanced at me, smirking. "Since you're still recovering, I'll take this one, but you owe me."

She strode out from behind the front desk and went over to Hank, shaking her head as she took in his flour-covered face. They walked into the bistro together, the door swinging shut behind them.

I stared at the bistro doors once I was alone, my mind whirling. Who was this person coming to see the inn? Why would they want to discuss the inn's financial future? Was Tracy trying to get rid of this place?

I TRIED to focus on the spreadsheets in front of me, but thoughts of Tracy and what she was up to wouldn't leave my mind. Thirty minutes later, she still hadn't returned from the bistro, so I left the front desk and decided to go to the clinic. I hoped Dr. Bennett would be willing to write up a new prescription for me to replace the pills I'd spilled at Cuppa Joe's that morning.

A rainstorm had rolled in at some point in the morning, so I slipped on my raincoat and hurried out to my car. I pulled out of the lot and headed toward the clinic, my thoughts returning to Tracy.

Why would Tracy set up a meeting with someone to talk about the future of the inn without running it past me first?

I was the owner and, even though I did view the two of us more like business partners, I should be the one setting up these kinds of meetings. Still, what reason would she have for scheduling a meeting like this without talking to me about it first? Was this some kind of interior designer who wanted to talk to us about changing the wallpaper in the rooms, or was it a real estate agent trying to sell the place? Why hadn't I hunted her down to get more answers?

Did Tracy want to sell the inn? When I'd first shown up in Pine Brook, she'd been worried that I was going to sell the Hemlock. And, for a while, that was my plan. But, over time, I'd learned to really love this place and working with her. I'd thought she'd felt the same way, but now it looked like she was thinking differently. Did she think I wasn't capable of running the inn? I was still learning, of course, but I thought I'd been doing well. Was she trying to leave the inn herself?

I pulled into the clinic parking lot, determined to put Tracy out of my mind while I focused on getting more pills from Dr. Bennett. He'd given me such a big warning about not taking too many when I first came by, and I was worried he'd be resistant to writing me another prescription so soon after the first one. I needed to not be distracted while I talked to him and could stress about Tracy later.

Two other cars were in the lot: a black BMW and a tan Honda Civic. One light was on through the glass doorway of the building, though other lights in the building were off. I tossed my raincoat back on and hurried out into the rain, hoping I hadn't arrived too early for the clinic to be open.

Inside, the waiting room was quiet. The TV was off, and the room was empty. At that same moment, Dr. Bennett came through the back door that led to the offices and examining rooms. He looked up at the sound of my approach.

"Simone. What are you doing here?" he asked, slowing his pace.

"Hi, Dr. Bennett. The door was unlocked, so I assumed you were open. I had a little mishap this morning and spilled all my pills. I was hoping you could write up another prescription."

"Hmm." He furrowed his brows. "Didn't I just give you a prescription? I can't imagine you've used up all the pills yet."

"I had an accident at Cuppa Joe's this morning and spilled the rest of the pills. I promise this isn't me trying to pull one over on you." I glanced down at the countertop as I talked, a large, black purse set a few feet away from me in the corner of the desk.

"Let me look up what I gave you last time." He tapped a few keys at the computer and pursed his lips while he read the screen.

"Isn't that Gayle's purse?" I asked, pointing to the purse on the counter. I'd recognized the Prada label—when I'd seen it earlier that day at Cuppa Joe's, I'd been surprised to see she had such an expensive purse. Now that I was standing closer, I could tell the purse was several years old, looking rough around the edges but still in great condition. She probably bought it years ago and had held onto it as long as she could.

"Yes," Dr. Bennett said slowly, looking up from the computer. "Yes, I think that does belong to Gayle. I didn't realize she was here. I've been working in my office all morning—she must've come in without me realizing it."

"I saw her car out front, too—the tan Honda? She was at the coffee shop this morning and saw me drop the pill bottle. You can ask her what happened."

"All right, I'll go see if I can find her. I'll ask her what she saw." He tapped a few more keys on the keyboard, then turned and went through the door again to the back of the clinic.

I leaned against the counter while I waited for him to return. I hoped Gayle would back up my story. She seemed like the kind of person who might want to make someone suffer for the sake of it, but she was also a nurse and probably didn't want to see anyone in any major pain. At least not if she could do anything about it.

"Oh, my God!" Dr. Bennett's shout came from the back room, terror in his voice. Without pausing to think about it, I rushed behind the counter and through the doors that led to the rest of the clinic.

I raced down the hallway that led to the examining rooms and offices, following after where his voice had come from. The last door at the end of the hallway was slightly open, and I pushed my way through. Dr. Bennett stood at the entrance to the room, his eyes wide and his face pale.

"What is it? Are you hurt?" I asked, but he simply shook his head and pointed across the room.

On the other side of the room, Gayle was slouched on the floor. Pills were scattered around her, and her eyes were blank and unseeing, staring up into the air. I was too far away to get a good look, but even from across the room, I could see that her face was puffy and her skin was purple. Liam hurried over to her side and pressed his fingers against her neck. He looked up at me, his eyes wide.

"She's dead," he said, his voice cracking.

6

A fter having stumbled onto my fair share of dead bodies, I was an expert at what to do next. While Dr. Bennett began performing CPR on Gayle, I put in a call to 911 and explained the situation.

"I'm not entirely sure what happened," I said. "I'm at the health clinic in Pine Brook, but the doctor looks like he's trying to help her." Dr. Bennett had pulled out an EpiPen from one of the drawers nearby and shoved it into Gayle's leg, but even I could tell that she wasn't getting up again.

The 911 operator asked to speak with Dr. Bennett since he was trying to assess the situation, and I stepped further away from Gayle's dead body after handing him the phone, wrapping my arms around myself to stop the shakes. Even after all the death I'd seen in this town, it still didn't get any easier.

"I injected her with an EpiPen, as her symptoms looked like anaphylactic shock," he said into the phone, sitting back on his heels on the ground. "I checked her airways and performed CPR, but I'm not sure what caused this. I thought the EpiPen might help, as I know Gayle has allergies, but she's not responding. You should send some EMTs out here as soon as you can."

I kept my gaze on the ground in front of me, even as his words filled the air around me. Gayle had been worried this morning that someone had put soy milk into her coffee because she was allergic to it. What else was she allergic to? Had she been exposed to something at the clinic?

There were pills scattered on the floor around her—had she taken something and overdosed? Gayle didn't seem like the kind of person to take a bunch of pills before her shift was about to start. More than likely, she'd been stocking up the pill bottles when the allergic reaction hit her and caused her to drop all the pills. A sob escaped me as I imagined Gayle back here, just trying to do her job, and instead dying alone and in pain. She was a grumpy woman, but that didn't mean she deserved to die like this.

"Yes, Dr. Bennett, that's right." The doctor's voice interrupted my tears. "I'm here with a patient, Simone Evans." He glanced over at me as the person on the line said something, but I couldn't read his expression.

"Yes, that Simone Evans," he said into the phone. "I guess you've heard of her."

My stomach dropped. In what world did 911 operators know who I was? Was I turning into that woman who kept finding dead bodies? One of these days, the police were going to start suspecting I was going around killing people just for the fun of it.

I slid my hands into my pockets and took a look around the room. I knew not to touch anything, even without being told by the police, but that didn't mean I couldn't look around.

This room was about the same size as the examining room I'd been in earlier that week, though obviously, this room served a different function. Cabinets lined the walls, full of different pill bottles. Gayle was slouched against the far wall, one of the cabinet doors open near her, and pills were scattered on the floor around her.

"Well, I wouldn't presume to know the cause of death from a brief examination," Dr. Bennett said into the phone, pulling my attention back to him. "But based on my experience and my knowledge of Gayle's health history, this looks like anaphylactic shock." He quickly ran through her symptoms, noting the blotchy skin and swollen features. "I know she had a severe soy allergy, but we'll need the medical examiner to make a final determination."

Apparently, Gayle wasn't being unreasonable this morning when she demanded to know if there was soy milk in her coffee. An allergy as severe as this would make anyone paranoid about the food and drink they ingested. I was ashamed of myself for having been so annoyed by Gayle's actions. She'd definitely thrown a temper tantrum at the coffee shop that morning, but was she right? Had someone put something in her coffee?

Dr. Bennett finished speaking with the 911 operator, hung up the phone, and passed it back to me. "They're sending EMTs and a patrol officer," he explained as I took the phone. "They said we shouldn't leave until they get here. The police are going to want to question us once they arrive."

Oh goody. More police interrogations. As if I didn't have enough of that in my life already. At least I was still feeling better, though I could feel a small knot of pain beginning to bloom in my lower back. I'd make sure to take one of the new pills from my refill as soon as I got home. Whenever that would be.

Dr. Bennett and I stood around the room in silence

while waiting for the police to arrive. He stood ramrod straight, wringing his hands together and glancing at his watch every few minutes. It must've been quite a shock to find one of his employees dead on the ground. He'd just told me a couple of days ago that he empathized with Gayle and thought she was good at her job. This must've been hard for him.

Still, was it possible that his hand-wringing and nervous glances were actually hiding a guilty conscience? I didn't know how Gayle had died and probably wouldn't know until the medical examiner had a chance to assess the situation, but Dr. Bennett had been alone with Gayle before I'd shown up. He'd said he didn't realize she was at the clinic and that he'd been alone in his office all morning, but was that a story he made up? He'd seemed surprised by my showing up here, so had he murdered Gayle when he thought they were alone?

I shook my head, exasperated at myself. A dead body didn't automatically mean murder! Just because I'd gotten caught up in a couple murder investigations in the past didn't mean that was what was happening here. I had enough things on my plate right now. I didn't need to get swept up in imagining a nefarious killer before anything had been proven. Besides, murder investigations and suspicious deaths were for the police to handle, not me.

About five minutes later, we heard footsteps in the hallway. Dr. Bennett went to the door and opened it to two EMTs, who rushed past him and went directly to Gayle's side. Two patrol officers followed them in.

I recognized Officer Scott instantly. We'd had our fair share of run-ins in the past; it seemed like he was always the first one at a crime scene, and, given that I had a habit of stumbling onto dead bodies, we'd spent a lot of time together at crime scenes. Oddly enough, I didn't actually know his first name.

"Both of you, please step back," Scott said, taking command of the room and motioning to Dr. Bennett and me to leave the room while the EMTs worked.

Dr. Bennett led me down the hallway to another room that was much larger and looked like a lunchroom for the employees of the clinic. A vending machine stood in the corner, and a microwave was on the countertop. Dr. Bennett glanced at his watch and ran a hand through his hair.

"We're expecting patients shortly. I'm going to see if I can turn them away while the police deal with everything." He didn't wait for a response, clearly speaking more to himself than to me, and left the room.

I took a seat at the table and clasped my hands together, trying to steady my breathing. All I could think about was the look on Gayle's face and how unnatural she'd looked in her final moments. I'd never had an allergic reaction to anything, save for some cheap lotion once when I was a kid, but it didn't look like a pleasant way to die.

A short while later, Officer Scott came into the lunch-room, his face ashen. Apparently, neither of us had gotten used to seeing dead bodies.

"Thanks for sticking around," he said, taking a seat across from me at the table. "I'd like to get your statement while you're here."

"Is she...is she dead?" My voice came out in a squeak, and I cleared my throat.

Scott nodded. "Dr. Bennett said he tried to perform CPR and injected her with an EpiPen, but none of that worked. Did you see him do that?"

I nodded. "He tried to do what he could to save her, but she must've been dead for longer than we realized."

"Got it." Scott pulled out a notepad and flipped to a clean page. "Tell me what happened here."

His voice had a commanding quality to it, and he held his pen steady. In the past, he'd nearly vomited at crime scenes, but he clearly had a better handle of things now.

"Dr. Bennett and I were in the reception area. I'd come early to ask him to write up a prescription for me. I'd gotten one earlier from him, but I'd accidentally dropped the pills at Cuppa Joe's this morning and needed a new prescription. He didn't want to write it at first, since he'd just given me one recently, but that's when I noticed Gayle's purse. She was at Cuppa Joe's this morning and saw me drop the pills. I told him he should go back and ask her to confirm. He went to the back, and I heard him shout a few minutes later. I rushed to the back, not even thinking about it, and that's when I found him standing over her body."

"How did you know it was Gayle's purse at the front desk?"

"I'd noticed it at the coffee shop. It hadn't seemed like the kind of purse Gayle would have. Fancy, but it wasn't just that. It was...ostentatious. Prada labels are pretty flashy. Gayle seemed like the kind of woman who wouldn't care about things like that. Dr. Bennett hadn't realized she was here, but I knew she must be since her purse was here."

"That purse could have belonged to anyone, though, even with the Prada label. How do you know for sure it was Gayle's?"

I thought for a moment, trying to remember what had led me to be so convinced that Gayle was in the building.

"I also remembered seeing her car in the parking lot. There are two other cars in the lot, besides mine—a BMW and a tan Honda. I figured the BMW belonged to Dr. Bennett— doctors seem to love BMWs—and I saw Gayle drive off in a tan Honda this morning. She must have come straight here from the coffee shop and gone into work."

"I see." Scott scribbled more notes into his notepad, his gaze down. "What happened once you got to the back room?"

"We called 911. Dr. Bennett checked for a pulse and tried to save her, but I think too much time had passed. The medical examiner will know for sure."

"Yes, Dr. Haynes is on her way," Scott said, scribbling in his notepad. "Did you know Gayle well?"

I shook my head. "Not really. As you know, I'm still new in town. I'd only met her recently when I needed to go to the doctor's. I got the sense she was...difficult to work with. She seemed grumpy most of the time."

Based on the interactions I'd seen already between Gayle and others, grumpy might've been an understatement. I didn't want to throw anyone under the bus, but if this did turn out to be murder, I felt it was my duty to make sure the police had all the information they needed.

"I did see her get into some...disagreements...with a few other people."

I told Officer Scott about seeing her berate Maria, blow up at Stella, and I even told him about her supposed history with Estelle. I felt bad about offering up my friend like this, but I knew from experience that it was bound to come up. Estelle wasn't a killer, so better to get what I knew out there rather than keeping it to myself and forcing the police to do the extra work of discovering it themselves. Who knew how long they'd keep Estelle on a suspect list if that happened?

"I'm not saying Gayle was killed, of course," I said hurriedly. "But if she was, there are probably several people you should talk to. Dr. Bennett seemed to like her, at least. Well, he told me she was misunderstood and that she was better once you got to know her. He kept employing her, so I guess she was good at her job."

Just then, the door to the room opened, and Detective Monica Patel poked her head into the room. She was wearing black slacks, a gray silk blouse, and a black blazer under a black trench coat. Her brown skin was flawless as usual, her piercing eyes taking in every inch of the room.

"I really should stop being surprised about finding you at these crime scenes," she said with a smirk as her gaze settled on me. I made a face, understanding how bad it looked that I kept stumbling onto dead bodies.

"If you didn't keep finding the killers for us, I'd be more worried," Patel added. "I guess some people just have all the bad luck." I tried not to think about what this type of bad luck meant for me.

"She doesn't find all the dead bodies," Scott piped up, finishing his notes. "What about that body found by the creek last week?"

Patel's face closed off, her detective eyes coming through. "You're right. Simone doesn't find all the dead bodies in town."

"I heard about that," I said, remembering what I'd read in the newspaper. "Sounds like it was an overdose?"

Patel nodded. "Drug usage has skyrocketed over the past thirty years in this country, and Pine Brook isn't immune from it." She turned back to Scott. "Are you done with your questions? I'd like for you to walk me through the crime scene. Maybe get Simone's take on things."

I held down the feeling of glee that popped up at Patel's words. While I wasn't a cop, I had helped with a lot of cases, and I was pleased to see that Patel was willing to get my perspective.

The three of us shuffled out of the lunchroom and back

to the room where Gayle's body was found. The hallway was now full of police personnel, and we had to squeeze past a few people to get to the room. Dr. Bennett was out in the hallway, speaking with another patrol cop, and our eyes met as I walked past.

"One moment," he said to the cop he'd been speaking with, then reached out a hand to stop me. "Here," he said, passing me a slip of paper. "I wrote up another prescription for you. I figured, now that Gayle is dead, she wouldn't be able to verify your story, but I don't want to see you in pain. Try not to lose these pills, okay?"

"I promise," I said, taking the slip of paper, grateful that he'd believed me. I followed Patel and Scott to the crime scene.

The back room had filled up in the time since we'd left. The county medical examiner, Dr. Haynes, kneeled over Gayle's body, studying the dead woman.

As soon as Patel entered the room, she took command of the scene. The various cops standing around all took a step back from what they were doing to let her walk through the room. Scott and I hurried after her, the room remaining parted for us.

One officer was dusting one of the counters for finger-prints, and another was bagging some material they'd found on the floor. Why were they treating this like a crime scene? Wasn't it an allergic reaction?

"Haynes, what have you got for me?" Patel asked, coming to a stop near Gayle's body.

The tall, blonde medical examiner stood from her kneeling position and cleared her throat. "My initial assess-ment had indicated foul play, given the location of the body and missing pills, as if someone had come in here while she was counting pills and tried to steal them."

She pointed over her shoulder to one of the cabinets, and Patel, Scott, and I all leaned to the side to see. One of the cabinet doors swung open, and it did look like something might be missing from the shelves, though it was hard to say because of all the pills scattered around Gayle.

"However, Dr. Bennett explained that no high-value pills are kept back here, and the pills scattered around the body are low-value items: naproxen, ibuprofen, that sort of thing. After a closer assessment of Ms. Hart's condition, I found no evidence of blunt force trauma. I'll need to get the body back to the county office for a complete autopsy, but my initial assessment is that this woman died of anaphylactic shock. Swollen face, discoloration of the skin, and a history of severe allergies all led me to this conclusion."

I let out the breath I hadn't realized I'd been holding. The whole time I'd been standing in the room with Gayle's dead body on the ground, I'd been so concerned that there was another murderer in town, especially given how grumpy Gayle was with everyone she met. Pine Brook had already had so many murders; could it handle another? But a fatal allergic reaction, while tragic, was not cause for concern.

"Thanks, doc," Patel said, pulling out her notepad and jotting down a few notes. "Since it's not foul play, we'll need to get next of kin's permission to do an autopsy, but I'm sure Justin will want to make sure we know exactly how Gayle died."

"Who's Justin?" I asked, unable to keep myself from butting in.

Three heads swiveled in my direction.

"Gayle's son," Patel said after a moment, apparently not minding my butting in. "He lives with her in town. We'll need to send someone to him to break the news."

"How do you know her son?"

Patel hesitated. "He's had some...run-ins with the police. Kid stuff, mostly, but in a town this small, all the cops get to know the local juveniles."

She made eye contact with Officer Scott, and the two had a moment of looking into each other's eyes. Were they communicating telepathically?

"All right, Ms. Evans, thank you for your time," Scott said, turning to me and beginning to usher me out of the room. Apparently, they had had a conversation without speaking, and the crux of that conversation was that I needed to leave now. "We'll be in touch to get a signature on your statement. And try to keep news of Ms. Hart's death to yourself until we've had a chance to speak with her son."

"Of course," I said, leaving the room.

The adrenaline wave I'd been riding since discovering Gayle was finally falling, and exhaustion was coming over me. It was still morning, but I felt like collapsing in bed and sleeping for days. The knot of pain in my back was gradually growing, and I was grateful Dr. Bennett had been thoughtful enough to write up a new prescription.

I was surprised that he was holding himself together right now. He'd seemed to be the only person in town who'd felt any kindness about Gayle, and now she was dead. I couldn't imagine what he must've been feeling right now. I was just grateful we didn't have another murder on our hands.

Oh, how wrong I would be.

7

I t was almost lunchtime as I drove back to the inn, but the images of Gayle's swollen face drilled into my brain kept my appetite far away. I wanted to put some distance between myself and the poor woman's death.

The inn was quiet as I entered the lobby. No sign of Tracy, but Lola came out to greet me and beg for pets. I rubbed her ears and snuck her a treat from behind the front desk. I rang Tracy on my cell phone as I flipped through the sign-in sheet on the front desk, checking to see which guests were still with us today.

No answer from Tracy. I frowned and left a message, asking her to call me back. I was still confused about this person she'd said was coming to the inn to discuss our future, and I needed to talk to her to figure out what was going on. I was jumping to conclusions by assuming that she was trying to make some big changes to the inn without talking to me first, but I couldn't do anything about it until we'd had a chance to speak. Hopefully, she'd show up later in the day.

The afternoon passed by quickly. Word of Gayle's death

hadn't yet been released, which meant I wasn't able to talk to anyone about what I'd seen yet. A few guests checked in and out, but mostly I was able to deal with paperwork and let my mind drift back to Gayle's tragic death.

Though a fatal allergic reaction wasn't necessarily suspicious—it could happen every day, to all kinds of people—I had to admit that the death of a woman like Gayle was going to be good news to some people. After all the ways I'd seen her treat the people around her, I had to wonder if any of them would've wanted her dead. It's possible many of them did, though of course that didn't mean they had killed her. But her death now was probably going to bring joy to some people in town. How tragic to live a life where your death makes others happy.

Did Gayle think about that in the moments she had before her allergic reaction pushed her over the edge? Did she regret the way she'd treated others? Was she happy with the way her life had turned out? Or did she think about her son and the fact that he would now be alone in the world without her? I was grateful that it wasn't my job to tell family members their loved one had died. That seemed like the worst part about Patel's job.

Suddenly, it was six o'clock, and Lola was ready to go home for the day. Tracy hadn't shown up at all, which was strange for her, but more than likely she'd be in bright and early the next day. I pulled out my phone to send her a text as Lola and I left the inn, but paused as I realized Tracy had texted me at some point in the day. I'd missed the notification.

Dealing with a family emergency. Need to leave town for a few days. I asked Nadia to come in to help out.

Oh, no. What family emergency was Tracy dealing with? I typed out a response to the message, sending good thoughts her way and asking her to tell me how I could help, then slipped my phone back into my pocket. That explained why she hadn't shown up today, and I hoped everything was okay with her.

On the drive home, my phone buzzed. A call from Nick. I put him on speakerphone, my smile wide across my face.

"How are you?" he asked, his voice filling my car.

"I'm okay. Kind of a chaotic day, but nothing I can't handle." I'd told the police I wouldn't say anything about Gayle's death until they'd had a chance to talk to her son, and I wanted to keep that promise.

"You'll have to tell me about it on our date. I ended up with some extra Brussels sprouts in my last harvest, and I thought I'd make us dinner, rather than going out somewhere. How does Friday night sound?"

"That sounds perfect," I said, my smile so wide it hurt my cheeks. "I'm looking forward to it."

"Awesome. Have a good night, okay?"

"You, too." I hung up the phone and tightened my hands on the wheel, joy streaming through me. The day had started out pretty tragically, but it was ending wonderfully, and I couldn't wait until our date.

THE NEXT DAY, I woke early, the sun barely cresting the horizon outside my window. I lay in bed for a few moments, blinking up at the ceiling. The events of the previous morning played through my head. Had Patel had a chance to talk to Gayle's son yet? Would news of her death spread around town now?

I'd managed to stop off at the pharmacy on the way home last night to get a refill, and I'd taken one of the pain pills before going to sleep. My back felt better this morning, and my mind was clear. Lola must've sensed I was awake because she perked up from the bottom of the bed and climbed up to lay next to me. She stuck her head on my chest, licking at my nose. I smiled and pushed her away.

"All right, all right, I'm up," I said, pushing the covers off and swinging my legs over the side of the bed to the ground.

I stretched, turning my neck this way and that, and stood. The pain pills were helping, as I felt a million times better today than I had in a week. The solid nine hours of sleep didn't hurt either.

I slipped my feet into slippers—the hardwood floors in this apartment, while glamorous, were icicles in the morning —and padded into the bathroom. Even though I was feeling better, I still couldn't get Gayle out of my head. Another death in this town, and it wasn't a murder. How strange was that?

At about eight o'clock, a knock came at my door. Pulling on my robe and checking on Lola to make sure she wouldn't flee through the doorway, I pulled it open to Estelle standing on the other side.

"Good morning, good morning!" She rushed past me, a ball of energy. "What a wild twenty-four hours you have had, my dear! Why didn't you call me immediately about the dead body?"

I cracked a half-smile and shut the front door. So much for my quiet morning of contemplation. Estelle couldn't keep herself away from death in this town; no wonder she'd found out about Gayle so soon after it happened.

"Coffee?" I asked, padding back into the kitchen. I'd figured I would pick up something for myself before heading into the inn, but now that Estelle was here, with no sign of leaving, I might as well make up a pot.

She nodded and pulled herself up onto one of the stools in the kitchen, leaning against the small marble island that divided up the room.

"Tell me everything that happened," she said, her voice now turning serious. It was her investigator's voice, without a doubt.

I poured coffee grounds into the coffee machine and pressed a button to get it brewing. "You're here so early," I said, resting my arms back against the countertop. "What if I was still asleep?"

She waved her hand flippantly. "I know you—every time you find a dead body, you're up early the next day. I guess it's hard to sleep with that image in your mind?"

Wow, she really did know me well. That was exactly what had happened with every other body I'd stumbled onto. I hadn't made the connection myself, but it probably would explain why I had a tendency to get dark circles under my eyes a few times a month. I wasn't sleeping! Of course, the pain pills this time had managed to knock me out, but would I have as good of sleep tonight? Only time would tell.

The coffee pot made a ding as it finished brewing, and I pulled two mugs down from the cabinet. I grabbed some milk from the fridge and a small, green ceramic pot from the counter where I kept the sugar and set them both on the island with the mugs. Once the coffee was ready, Estelle and I prepared our cups, the scent of the dark roast wafting into the air between us.

"I suppose you've heard that it was Gayle," I said, glancing up at her as we poured coffee into our mugs.

Estelle nodded. I gave my head a shake and chuckled. Was Detective Patel aware of how easily this information got out to the public? Had Gayle's son even been notified before Estelle found out?

"Don't worry," Estelle said as if reading my mind. "Someone told her son before I was told. I only found out about it because I ran into Miriam at the grocery store this morning, and she couldn't wait to spill the beans."

Estelle's hairdresser's mother worked at the police station in some kind of role that meant she always got lots of information about current cases. Miriam seemed to have more information than she should've at any given point, but I didn't want to question our source.

"It's lucky I ran into Miriam because, for some reason, my best friend didn't think I needed to know what had happened." Estelle narrowed her eyes sternly, though she couldn't help a smile peeking through.

"Sorry," I said, grimacing. "The police didn't want me to say anything until her son was notified. Besides, I didn't think allergic reactions would interest you that much. I came straight home and fell right asleep."

"It's no matter," she said with a wave of her hand. "I'm here now, so you can tell me all about it."

"What's there to say?" I asked, taking a sip of my coffee. It wasn't as good as Hank's or what I could get at Cuppa Joe's, but it was good enough for me right now. "The medical examiner thinks it was anaphylactic shock. Nothing nefarious."

"Did the medical examiner say for sure that's what happened?"

I shifted my weight between my feet, thinking back to the night before. "Well, no. It's all preliminary right now. I guess they need to get permission from her son about doing an autopsy, and then we'll know for sure."

"Which means it could've been something more nefarious, right? We should keep our options open. You met Gayle; she made enemies wherever she went. It's not a stretch to think that someone did this to her intentionally."

"I mean, I guess, but it could've been an accident, right?"

"Maybe. I'm just saying, we shouldn't assume we know what happened until the final report is given on her death. We can't let the real killer get away, if there is one."

"What about you and Gayle? What was your relationship like? Why didn't you like each other?"

Estelle tried to brush away the question like a bothersome fly, but she couldn't hide the way her body tensed up. "It's old history. We weren't close, that's true, but I honestly didn't think about her most of the time. She was the worst part about going to that clinic, though. I always tried to make appointments when I knew it was her lunchtime or when she was away on vacation, which wasn't very often."

Estelle must've liked Dr. Bennett a lot to continue going to him even though Gayle was his nurse. She was bound to have some appointments where she had to see Gayle, and the two of them would be stuck behind closed doors while Gayle prodded her with medical devices. What did they talk about while they were back there?

"What do you think of Dr. Bennett?" I asked her. "He said he thought Gayle was really effective, even if her bedside manner left something to be desired. I was surprised that he would keep her employed, given how nasty she was to everyone who came in."

Estelle shrugged, cradling her mug. "That was probably the one decision he made that I couldn't agree with. Dr. Bennett's lived in Pine Brook his whole life. He left for a few years for medical school and training in a bigger city, but came back about ten years ago when his parents got sick. He and Deborah, that's Dr. Li, they set up the clinic then.

They'd known each other in high school; I think they might've dated, actually. When they both became doctors, it seemed like an easy choice to join forces in a town of this size."

Dr. Bennett and Dr. Li had dated? Granted, it was in high school, but still. I couldn't imagine starting a business with an old romantic entanglement. Seemed like a recipe for disaster. Of course, my romantic entanglements had a habit of ending in cheating and shouting matches, so maybe I wasn't the best example to pull from.

"I wonder who they're going to get to replace Gayle," I asked, finishing up my cup of coffee. "Are there a lot of nurses in town looking for work?"

Estelle shrugged. "Probably. I bet there are some that commute into Seattle or Tacoma, and would love the chance to stay local. I'd be interested to see who they find, too. Anyone is bound to be better than Gayle."

Estelle set down her coffee mug and reached into her purse. She began digging around while I put our empty mugs in the sink. Moments later, she dumped the contents of her purse onto the island.

"What are you doing?" I asked, hurrying over to stop the things from falling on the floor

"My supplements," she said, looking up, her eyes wide. "I can't find them."

"Well, maybe you left them at home." I wiped down the counter with a washcloth as I spoke. "I'm sure they'll turn up."

"I hope so." Estelle stood, shoving all of her belongings back into her purse. "I'll let you finish getting ready. Let's meet for lunch at the inn, if you're feeling up to it?"

"Sounds like a plan."

THE INN WAS quiet when I arrived later that morning. We had a few guests checked in and a couple checking out that day. Tracy and I had spent some time recently discussing how to increase revenue for the inn during the quieter season after the holidays but before the weather turned warm and tourists flocked to town. She and Aunt Sylvia had tried out different things over the years—holding contests, parties, things like that—but they hadn't found anything that stuck. I'd promised Tracy I would keep thinking of ideas that would work every year.

Lola was happy to be back at the inn. I let her off her leash at the front door, and she bounded into the lobby, sniffing at every nook and cranny she could get her nose into. After a few moments, satisfied that she'd found every new smell that had appeared since she'd last been here, she trotted over to her bed behind the front desk, spun around on it a couple of times, then collapsed with a sigh and closed her eyes.

I went behind the front desk and pulled up the ledger for that week. Like I remembered, things were quiet this week. I made a few notes in the ledger about guests who had previously checked out and made sure everything was up to date. I sent Estelle a text, asking if she'd found her supplements. She sent back a *No* very quickly. I considered calling her to see how she was doing when the front door of the inn opened.

A woman walked in. Her face was familiar, though it took me a second to place her. She strode to the front desk and after a moment, I recognized her as the woman I'd spilled soapy water on earlier in the week.

"Hello, I'm looking for Tracy," she said once she was at the front desk.

"Can I just say how sorry I am about what I did with the water? I hope it didn't ruin your nice clothes." I looked her up and down, gulping at the invisible price tags. "Do you need me to pay for the dry-cleaning bill?"

She laughed, her eyes sparkling. "Not at all, dear. It's no trouble. Is Tracy around? We had a meeting scheduled for this morning."

Was this the woman Tracy wanted us to meet with about the financial future of the inn? "I'm sorry, Tracy's not around right now," I said after a moment of awkward silence. Why hadn't Tracy given me any more information about this woman? "As the inn's owner, I'd be happy to talk with you about what you two have discussed."

The woman paused, studying me, then pulled a thick business card out of her purse and passed it across the desk. "I think it's probably best if we wait until Tracy is around," she said. "She said she wanted us all to be at this meeting. Please give me a call once Tracy is available." She gave a tiny wave, then left the inn.

I stared at the card in my hand. *Isabella Rodriguez, Investor* was typed across the front. Investor?

I turned away from the front desk and pulled out my cell phone, quickly dialing Tracy's number. The phone rang twice, then went to voicemail. Drat. Why wasn't Tracy answering her phone? I knew she was dealing with a family emergency, but it wasn't like her not to answer her phone and tell me what was going on, especially if she had a meeting scheduled at the inn. I sent off a text, asking her to call me, and slipped my phone back into my pocket. Isabella's card was heavy in my hand. What was Tracy up to?

_____

8

The rest of the day passed quickly. Tracy never showed up, so I wasn't able to get my questions answered about this Isabella person. Given that Isabella was an investor, it was more likely that Tracy was trying to expand the inn, rather than sell it out from under me. Still, why hadn't she talked to me about this first? Even if we were business partners, Tracy shouldn't be scheduling meetings without talking to me. And now she was gone and not answering my calls, so I couldn't even yell at her about it!

Nadia ended up showing up for her shift, so I was able to get a break from the front desk. I went back to the office and did some paperwork, still stewing over Tracy. I also couldn't stop thinking about Gayle. It was sad to lose any life, no matter how grumpy they might be, and now her son was all alone. It was such a tragic situation.

Around lunchtime, Estelle and I met in the bistro as planned. We ordered the special from Penny and sat back in our seats to wait for the food.

"Did you ever find your supplements?" I asked.

Estelle shook her head. "I'm not sure what happened to them. It's so strange. I've been taking those pills for years, and I've never lost them before. I don't know how I managed to misplace them now."

I reached over and squeezed her hand, surprised at the emotion in her voice. Was she worried that she was starting to forget things? Had she forgotten other things recently? Estelle wasn't a spring chicken anymore, but I'd never known her to be forgetful. Of course, I'd only known her for a few months, but it felt like longer than that, given our shenanigans.

"Can Dr. Bennett write up another prescription for you?"

"It's not so much a prescription, as just calling in an order with his supplier. I'll try to stop by the clinic later to see if he can help, but I know they've been swamped since Gayle's death. I don't want to create more work for them right now."

"Maybe they'll turn up in the meantime. Don't worry, it'll be okay."

Penny brought out our food, and Estelle and I dug in, turning the conversation to other topics. Penny hung around and chatted with us, as there weren't many guests in the dining room right now. We were laughing at something Penny had said when the door to the bistro swung open, and in walked Patel with two patrol officers behind her. Our laughter died down quickly at the sight.

"What's going on?" I asked, standing up and taking a step towards the police. Had there been another murder?

Patel held up her hand to stop my progression. "We're not here for you, Simone," she said, her gaze shifting to Estelle. "Mrs. Adler, we were hoping we could take you down to the station for a few questions."

Estelle gave a squeak, and I stepped in front of her as if my presence could possibly stop these police officers from taking her anywhere they wanted to.

"What's this about?" I asked. "She has a right to know what this is regarding."

Patel sighed. "Some information has come out in regard to the death of Gayle Hart, and we're now looking into it as a suspicious death. We'd like to speak with Mrs. Adler to see if she has any pertinent information to share."

My stomach plunged. Not again. I didn't want to watch another friend get dragged down to the police station for questioning.

"Why can't you speak with her here? We've got a perfectly good courtyard that's great for questioning people." I didn't add that Patel already knew that since she'd questioned me many times there, but she seemed to have read my mind as her eyes narrowed.

"We need to go down to the station," she said firmly. "May I speak with you for a moment?" she added, motioning with her head to the side.

The two other police officers walked over to Estelle. She rose to her feet, gulped hard, and followed them out of the room. The rest of the bistro was silent. I watched them go, then turned my anger onto Patel.

"What is wrong with you? Why would you take her out of here like that? The courtyard is perfectly acceptable, and—"

"Please keep your voice down," Patel said, pulling me over to the back of the dining room, away from the other guests and closer to the kitchen door. "We're not arresting her," she said, dropping her voice to keep others from overhearing. "We just have some questions for her, but it'll be easier to do that at the station. I'd rather not put Estelle on display in the courtyard with police officers standing around. At the station, she'll have some privacy."

At least she was looking out for Estelle's reputation. Still, I wasn't going to let her take my friend without a fight.

"What information has come out about Gayle's death? I thought it was an allergic reaction?" I asked.

"So did we," Patel said. "But the M.E. found soy in Gayle's system after the preliminary toxicology report, and we found a pill bottle with soy supplements inside at the crime scene after you left. The bottle had Estelle's name on it. We'd like to understand how that bottle ended up in the back room with Gayle."

"Wait, Estelle lost her pills," I said, remembering what we'd just been talking about. "She hasn't seen them for a couple of days. Someone might've taken them from her and left them behind at the crime scene. The real killer could be framing Estelle!"

Patel studied me, narrowing her eyes as if calculating the merits of what I'd said, then she pulled out her cell phone and typed out a note.

"I'll be sure to ask her about the missing pills," she said, putting her phone back into her pocket. "I need to go, and you need to stay here. Estelle isn't in trouble right now, but if you start sticking your nose into places it doesn't belong, it may not bode well for her." She sighed, her energy level deflating. "Honestly, we're pretty understaffed right now at the police station, and I'm just doing the best I can to stay above water with this investigation. I need you to let me do my job, okay?" She spun on her heel and strode out of the bistro, not waiting for a response from me.

I took a couple of deep breaths as I stood there, trying to calm myself. Patel was a good cop; I'd seen that many times in the past. She wasn't likely to arrest Estelle for something she didn't do. If Gayle had been killed, possibly poisoned by soy, then Patel would find the right killer.

I knew Estelle was innocent, just like I knew Lola loved dog treats. There was no doubt about it. Me running off, half-cocked and claiming police brutality because they brought in a little old lady for questioning, wouldn't get us anywhere. I pushed open the door to the kitchen and stepped inside, away from the prying eyes of the guests in the bistro.

Unfortunately, the eyes in the kitchen were just as prying. They tried to hide it, but Hank spun away as soon as I entered; Javier started whistling and sweeping; and Eddy, one of the servers, picked up two plates he'd undoubtedly set down when he heard the commotion outside. He glided past me, smiling as he went, and continued on to deliver the food.

"What's going on?" Hank asked, unable to keep his question to himself.

I sighed and walked over to him, grabbing a french fry off a plate for a guest. I couldn't help myself, either. "Did you hear about that nurse who died?" I asked him, popping the french fry into my mouth. "Gayle Hart?" I wouldn't normally talk to Hank about murder, but my usual sidekick was down at the police station and Tracy was nowhere to be found. I needed to talk to someone about what was going on, and Hank was my best option right now.

He nodded, his head bobbing. "Of course. It's all over town. I heard it was an allergic reaction. What are the police doing here?"

"Apparently, she was poisoned," I said, leaning against the countertop. "I shouldn't say much more, but I guess they had some questions for Estelle."

Hank's eyes widened and his cheeks turned pink. He

always hated murder investigations, but he was clearly living in the wrong town if that was how he felt.

"Well, I'm sure it's all just a misunderstanding." He began grating cheese over a plate of pasta to keep his hands busy. "Estelle would never do anything like that."

"I'm sure they'll clear everything up."

Just because the police were asking Estelle some questions, didn't mean they'd arrest her for murder. Patel was a good cop, and they'd find the killer eventually. But how long would they keep the suspicion on Estelle until they did? Patel had admitted she was understaffed; how much longer would it take her to solve this thing if she didn't have the support she needed?

Estelle's pill bottle at the crime scene was not a good sign. Plus, the way Gayle had been so harsh about Estelle when I'd brought her up; there was clearly history between the two women. Had the police uncovered the truth of what had gone on between the two of them? This town was full of gossips, and I didn't want to see Estelle bearing the brunt of it while the police tried to find the real killer. I had no choice now—I had to help find the killer to save my friend.

"I need to call Miles," I said to Hank, pushing away from the counter. Estelle's husband needed to know what was going on. "Thanks for the fries," I added, swiping another one off the same plate as I left the kitchen.

I slipped my phone out of my pocket and found Miles' number, hating that I'd now found myself smack dab in the middle of another murder investigation. Where would I even start?

9

"Yes, I think it would be good if you went down to the station and met her," I said into my phone, now out in the lobby and sitting in one of the armchairs. I'd gotten ahold of Miles and had broken the news to him about what had happened with his wife.

"Oh dear," he said, and I could picture him on the other end of the line, his white hair sticking up from his head, clutching the phone tightly. "Do you think she'll be okay? Does she need a lawyer?"

"I'm not really sure," I said. Would a lawyer make the police think she was more suspicious than she actually was? Or was a lawyer necessary to keep her safe during the questioning?

"Why don't you give Ron a call and see what he thinks?" I said to Miles, referring to Ron Chapman, the inn's lawyer and a close friend. He'd helped out in the past when the people I cared about had been accused of murder, and I was sure he'd want to help the Adlers as much as he could. "He could meet you down at the station and probably get some more information about what's going on. I'd come too, but I need to stay at the inn and keep an eye on things."

"Oh, no, no, don't worry about that," Miles said hurriedly. "I don't want you to stress out about all of this. I'm sure it's just a misunderstanding. I'll call Ron and do as you said."

We promised to stay in touch as things progressed, and then I hung up. Slipping my phone back into my pocket, I stood and went to the front door to grab my jacket. Nadia was still at the front desk, scheduled to be there for the next few hours at least. I slipped out the front door and headed to my car.

I hadn't been totally honest with Miles on the phone. It didn't make sense for me to meet them at the station since I wasn't likely to get any more information about Estelle than Ron was, and my presence might just anger the police chief, Tate. We'd had some run-ins in the past, and he didn't like me very much.

But I had lied to Miles about staying at the inn. I knew Nadia could handle things on her own for now. What I didn't want to do was hang around and wait for Tracy to show up, when all I could think about was how it seemed like she was trying to undermine me by bringing in this Isabella woman without talking to me about it first.

The best use of my time right now was to start getting answers about Gayle's death. If the police were so focused on Estelle, they might stop searching for the real killer. I, however, would go right to the last place Gayle had been seen alive: the health clinic.

I didn't know anything about Gayle's home life, but maybe someone at her job could help me figure out who might've wanted her dead. I wanted to save my friend, and

Patel had admitted she needed help with this case. I'd do what I could to help them both.

Traffic was light as I drove. It was mid-week, so people were either at work or at home. Though I was ostensibly doing this to help keep Estelle out of jail, a tiny part of me was thrilled to be back in the middle of another murder investigation.

I pulled into the parking lot of the office twenty minutes later. Police tape was strung across the door to the building. Drat. I forgot that the whole office would now be a crime scene. Would anyone be around for me to talk to?

Fortunately, there were a few cars in the parking lot. Even if they weren't seeing patients right now, someone who worked with Gayle would be around to speak with me.

I peeked over my shoulder as I approached the police tape, then swung underneath it and entered the building. Was it illegal to cross police tape if no one saw it?

Inside, the hallway was quiet as I walked down to the waiting room. I'd walked this same path only the day before; that day had ended much differently than I expected. Let's hope this excursion didn't turn out quite the same.

The waiting room was empty, no surprise there, but fortunately, Maria was seated behind the front desk, tapping away at her computer. She jumped when I pushed open the door to the waiting room.

"Sorry." I smiled, trying to appear friendly, and approached the front desk. "Didn't mean to scare you."

"It's okay." Her smile couldn't hide the exhaustion in her eyes. "I don't think you're supposed to be here," she said with a look over her shoulder to the back office.

"Are the police still here?"

"No, but they told us not to let any patients come in.

They put up tape and everything at the front door. Didn't you see it?"

"No, I did, but I'm not here as a patient." They should've locked the front door if they wanted to keep people out.

"I wanted to stop by and see how everyone was doing," I went on. "It must've been quite a shock to learn Gayle was dead. How are you holding up?"

Maria sagged under the weight of my question, the perky veneer she'd kept up now fading. "It really is surprising. I didn't want to come in today, but Dr. Bennett said it was important to keep this place running. He thought that's what Gayle would have wanted. We have to find a new nurse now, so I've been placing job ads online." She gestured to her computer.

I nodded, murmuring my understanding, while silently processing what she'd said. Dr. Bennett wanted Maria to work today? You'd think he'd give his employee the day off after another employee had been found dead in the office. But I supposed he was right that it was important to keep the ship running.

A small flag sat next to Maria's computer. Red and white alternating stripes, with a blue triangle on the side and a white star in the middle of the triangle. Where was that from?

"It's the Puerto Rican flag," Maria said, noticing me looking at it. She straightened the little flag on its stand, though it was already as straight as she could make it. "It's where I'm from. I came to Washington when I was a teenager."

"It's beautiful." I didn't know much about the U.S. territory, but it was obvious that Maria was proud of her heritage.

"Is Dr. Bennett here?" I asked, glancing to the back

offices again. "Or Dr. Li? I was hoping to talk to someone about what happened to Gayle."

"Why?" Maria asked. "I thought it was an allergic reaction."

"Well, the police aren't so sure about that," I said slowly. I expected news of Estelle being taken in for questioning would've been all around town by now, but apparently not. Would Patel appreciate me revealing this information to others? Too late now.

Maria gasped. "What are you talking about? What happened?"

I sighed and glanced around, but we were still alone. "I heard there might have been foul play. I don't have any details, but I wanted to come by to see if anyone knew anything. You've worked here for a while, right? Did you know Gayle well?"

I had no clue if Maria had worked at the doctor's office for a while, but her comfort with the doctors and the assorted personal items scattered across the front desk made me think she'd been around for a long time. The real question was: did she have strong feelings about Gayle?

"Not very well," Maria said, her gaze down. "Nurses don't really interact much with the front receptionist. Mostly just with the doctors."

I'd seen Gayle berating Maria about some work thing. It had sounded like they worked together quite a bit, and Gayle wasn't happy about it. Was Maria now simply trying to distance herself because she didn't like Gayle, or was she hiding her murderous actions?

"Do you know much about her family life? I understand she had a son. Do you know where he lives?" I asked.

Maria shook her head hurriedly. "No. Like I said, we weren't very close. Gayle mostly kept to herself."

"I'll bet you have her address written down somewhere, in her file, maybe?" I pointed to her computer. "Could I see it? I just want to try to get some answers for her family, and it would help to talk to the people who knew her well."

"I'm sorry, I don't think I can share that." Her eyes darted around the room, looking anywhere but at me.

Why were these questions making her so uncomfortable? It was reasonable that she couldn't share personal employee information with me, which I understood—I'd only asked to see if she would do it. Still, her nerves seemed extreme for what I was asking.

Was she just surprised to learn that Gayle hadn't died of an allergic reaction? Was she uncomfortable because I was asking about Gayle's life? Or was she trying to hide a guilty conscience?

Switching tactics might help here. "Can you think of any reason why someone might want to hurt Gayle? I didn't know her well, either, but I saw her around town a few times, and it seemed like she made it a habit of pissing people off. Plus, she wasn't exactly Nurse Nightingale with me." More like Nurse Ratched. I made sure not to mention that Maria was one of the people I'd seen Gayle piss off.

"I'm sorry, I don't know anything." Maria stood abruptly, almost knocking over her desk chair. She looked around as if trying to find some way to save herself, then darted through the back door, bumping into Dr. Bennett as he came out into the waiting room, almost knocking him over.

What was that all about?

10

"Simone! Nice to see you. What are you doing here? We cancelled all of our appointments for the day," Dr. Bennett said after recovering from Maria's blast past him.

"Hi, Dr. Bennett. I was just stopping by to see how everyone was doing. Is Maria okay? She ran off in a hurry."

He glanced back through the back door, then turned back to me, coming over to the front desk. "She's been a little jumpy. Gayle's death is getting to her, which is understandable, but I think it's important that we keep working through this. Oh, and please, call me Liam. Dr. Bennett always feels so stuffy. We like to be more casual here. How are you doing?"

"I'm okay. Those pain pills are helping, though I'm trying to take it easy today. I'm definitely a little freaked out after yesterday, though. It's never easy seeing a dead body like that. I bet you're more used to it, right? As a doctor?"

He laughed, his charm practically oozing out of his pores. I found myself taking a step closer to the front desk just to get a little closer to him.

"Most of my patients are alive, fortunately," he said. "Dr. Li actually handles more of our geriatric patients, though I don't think she sees many dead people. I understand you've probably seen more dead bodies than us, huh? I've heard about your investigations around town."

His tone was teasing and kind, but I still found my cheeks warming. I didn't really want to become known as Pine Brook's amateur sleuth. I couldn't help it if murder investigations kept falling into my lap.

"That's actually why I'm here," I said, looking for any way to change the subject away from my purported sleuthing. "I'm not sure if you've heard, but the police think there may have been foul play with Gayle's death. Apparently, some pills were found in her system that caused the allergic reaction."

Liam's smile dropped, and he glanced down, shuffling a stack of papers in front of him. "Yes, I'd heard about that. Very dreadful news."

"The police found Estelle's soy supplements at the crime scene after I left. They think she intentionally poisoned Gayle with her pills."

"Oh, that's really tragic," he said, furrowing his brow. "I knew the two women didn't like each other much, but I never would've expected Estelle to be a killer."

"I'm not so sure that that's what happened," I said quickly. "Estelle is certain she lost those pills recently. Can you think of any reason why anyone else would've wanted to kill Gayle? Did she have any enemies?"

Liam cracked a smile at that but tried to cover it up. "Sorry. I know she's dead, and this is all very serious, but Gayle wasn't what you'd call a people-pleaser. I mean, you saw her when you were here. Grumpiness was her default mode."

"Still, you kept her employed, even knowing that she was short with patients. Why?"

"Like I said before, she was good at her job. Very efficient. Actually, kids seemed to like her a lot, and most patients eventually warmed up to her. I know not everyone here at the clinic liked working with her. But she was a single mother, had been for years. Dr. Li, Deborah, and I never had the heart to fire her."

I'd never met a business owner who was so willing to keep an employee on staff, even though they angered all the people who came into the business, simply because they had a tough home life. Heck, my previous boss, Antonio, had fired me for getting too aggressive with customers before coming to Pine Brook. Was Liam really that kind, or was there some other reason he wouldn't fire Gayle? Did she have something on him?

"Have the police had a chance to talk to you again?"

Liam nodded. "They stopped by this morning. That's when they put up the police tape. They wanted to know if we could think of anyone who might want to kill Gayle or if we had any reason to be involved. I told them I didn't know much. Gayle was just an employee. I think they may have their work cut out for them since so many people disliked her."

Estelle's pills were found at the crime scene and she had a dark history with Gayle, so the police had one suspect who seemed the most viable. I needed to find someone else for them to focus their attention on instead.

"Do you think they suspected that anyone here was involved?" I asked. "You or Dr. Li or Maria?"

Liam shrugged. "Maybe. My understanding is that everyone is a suspect this early in an investigation, until they find someone that seems most likely. But, based on the questions they asked, it doesn't seem like they suspect anyone in particular at this point."

Liam shifted his weight around, reshuffling the stack of papers he'd just shuffled. He flicked his gaze up to me briefly, then back down to the papers.

"What is it?" If he had something to say, he needed to just say it.

He sighed. "I hate to say this because I don't think he had anything to do with it...but you might consider talking to Gayle's son, Justin. They lived together in town for as long as any of us can remember. He's...not a great person."

Last night, Patel had mentioned that Justin had had some run-ins with the police. This guy was quickly moving to the head of my list of suspects.

"I don't want to make any judgments on him," Liam went on, "but I know he and his mother fought a lot. I actually think they got into a big argument last week. Justin had stopped by the office to talk to his mom, and even though she took him into one of the back offices, we could hear them shouting. Something about not giving him the money he needed. It was hard to understand, but they were both very angry. He left, muttering under his breath, and Gayle spent the rest of the afternoon in a bad mood. I tried to talk to her about it, tried to see if I could help, but she wouldn't say anything."

Liam sighed and rubbed the back of his neck. "I don't know if Justin has it in him to hurt his mom. I remember when he was a little kid, he was always so inquisitive and wanted to learn about all the doctor stuff we did in the office. I really thought he'd go off and do great things, but instead..." Liam looked up at me then. "I'm not saying he had anything to do with this, but if you're trying to get to the truth, you might want to talk to him."

I nodded, turning over this clue in my head. I'd wanted to do what I could to find Gayle's killer so that the police wouldn't suspect Estelle anymore, but I wasn't thrilled at the prospect of questioning someone who'd just lost their mother.

Also, why was Liam sharing so much with me about the personal lives of his employees? Was he trying to keep suspicion off of himself by serving up Gayle's son on a platter? Or was he just another town resident who couldn't keep their mouth shut when it came to the drama in other people's lives?

A thought came to me. "*Why* would Justin kill his mother? You said they didn't get along, but if we assume that Gayle was killed because she was exposed to soy, then it was probably premeditated, right? What reason would Justin have for murdering his mother in such a planned out way?"

Liam cocked his head to the side, thinking for a moment. "That's a good point. I hadn't thought of that. I didn't know much about their home life. Only that they would argue a lot. Maybe some fight started in the home which led Justin to want to murder her?"

"Do you know if she had money?" An inheritance could be a reason for murder.

Liam shrugged. "I didn't know much about her financial situation. She wasn't one to flash nice things around town. You'd probably have to talk to the police about any money she left behind."

Her Prada purse was the only indication I'd seen of wealth, and the purse had definitely looked a few years old. Unless Gayle was hiding her wealth, it wasn't a valid motive for Justin. And I wasn't looking forward to questioning a grieving son. I wanted to see how things were going on at the inn and see if Tracy had checked in yet, so I'd stop off there before rushing off to question Justin.

"I should probably let you get back to work," I said. "Thanks for talking to me."

"Of course," Liam said. "One last thing, Simone. Just be careful, okay? If someone did kill Gayle, you would be wise not to get in their way."

"I'll be careful," I said with a smile, exiting the building, his words still ringing in my head.

He was right that this could be dangerous, and it would be smart for me to not let many people know what I was doing. I wasn't interested in another face-off with a killer.

11

"I heard about Estelle," Nadia said as I walked through the inn doors into the lobby. "Is she going to end up in jail?"

"Hush," I said, hurrying across the lobby to the front desk. "Please don't spread any rumors around about what may or may not happen to Estelle. She's going to be fine."

"If you say so." She turned her attention back to the magazine on the counter in front of her, leaning her hip against the front desk.

"Anything interesting happen while I was gone?" I picked up the stack of mail laying on the counter and began flipping through the envelopes.

Nadia shook her head. "Well, one of the toilets overflowed, and a guest got into an argument with another guest about a table in the bistro. I guess they both thought they were sitting at the same table, and so they started yelling at each other about it."

Nadia had a habit of finding the chaos of the inn much less important than she should. "Are the guests okay?" I asked, starting to walk back around the desk and to the bistro doors.

"Oh, yeah, everything's fine," she said, waving her hand flippantly. "Hank offered them free drinks at dinner tonight, and everyone was happy."

"Phew. It's not a good look having guests fighting with each other. Have you heard from Tracy today?"

"Nope."

Drat. I'd hoped that she'd left another message explaining where she was and when she'd be back.

I stepped away from the desk, dialing her number, but it went straight to voicemail again. Was she avoiding my calls? Was this all part of her plan to undermine me and try to take over the inn?

I shook my head to clear my thoughts. These anxious thoughts weren't getting me anywhere, and neither was standing around the inn when nothing was going on and I wasn't needed.

"I have to run out again. Are you going to be okay here on your own?"

"It'll be a piece of cake," Nadia said, not once looking up from her magazine. Who knew they could be so engrossing?

I tossed the junk mail I'd been flipping through into the trash, gave Lola's ears a ruffle, and headed back outside to go find Justin, Gayle's son. I didn't want to question a grieving son, but I also didn't want to stew at the inn. This way, I could at least feel like I was doing something to help Estelle.

Once I was in my car, I called Miriam to see if she knew where Gayle and Justin lived. She gave me directions to their house and promised to call with any updates on Estelle. I turned on the engine and pulled out of the inn's parking lot.

Gayle and Justin lived across town in a neighborhood I

hadn't been to before. Small homes dotted the street, all close together. Most had a tiny patch of yard in the front, with tall fences along the back indicating more yard space. These were single-family houses, with varying degrees of care given to tending to the outside of each. They weren't extravagant homes, further dismissing the notion that Gayle had wealth that would go straight to Justin, but I didn't want to make any assumptions before I got more information about the two of them and their lives.

I pulled up in front of Gayle's house and parked across the street so I wouldn't be spotted if Justin happened to look out the window. I didn't know if he'd be home right now, but I was taking a chance he would be around. There was a black Toyota parked in the driveway. Gayle's tan Honda had been at the crime scene yesterday and was probably with the police right now. That meant that this Toyota was likely Justin's, and it looked like he might've been home.

Their front yard was disorganized and overgrown. The paint on the ramshackle house was peeling in places, and the grass was taller than all the other lawns on the block. Clearly, gardeners didn't live here.

I turned off the engine and pulled out my phone, quickly tapping out a text message to Estelle, letting her know where I was and what I was doing. I figured if Justin had killed his mother and decided to kill me for snooping around, I'd want someone to know what I was up to.

You could just as easily not go in there, a tiny voice in my head said, but I pushed it aside. It wasn't the first time I'd faced a suspected killer, or an actual killer, for that matter, and I had my friend to think about. Besides, from the way Liam described him, Justin sounded more like a loser than a killer. Yelling at your mom at her place of work, then going home and undoubtedly expecting her to cook you dinner after didn't sound like a killer to me. But I'd find out the truth shortly.

Three steps led up to the front door. I could see the original wood of the house peeking through the cracked paint, and the screen in the window to the left of the door was split. I knocked on the door and waited. As I stood, a tinge of pain shot up my back. I groaned and stretched to the side. Would this back pain ever go away?

The other homes on the street were quiet, though that wasn't surprising given the time of day. Still, was this street ever busy? Or did people mostly stay inside their houses?

Someone pulled open the door and stuck their head through the crack. A waft of weed poured out through the door, and I held my breath to keep from breathing anything in. Guess I knew what Justin was doing to mourn his mother's death. If my back pain got any worse, I could probably ask him to share a little with me.

"Yeah?" he asked, his voice higher-pitched than I expected. He was not much taller than me, his brown hair worn long and scraggly. His thin arms poked out from a white tank top, and his blue jeans were about two sizes too big. A leather belt was the only thing keeping them on his waist. Behind him, the house was dark.

"Justin Hart? My name is Simone. I was hoping to talk to you about your mother." I held out the bouquet of flowers I'd picked up at the grocery store before coming to his house. If I was going to try to question the kid about his mother's death, I may as well show up with something.

"Yeah? What about her?" He crossed his arms over his chest and shifted slightly in the doorway, giving me a glimpse into his house. A terrarium was situated against the far wall, though I was too far away to see what was inside. A TV flickered in the darkness. What was he watching?

"I heard about your mother. I wanted to extend my sympathies and check on you. Have the police talked to you today?"

"They came by this morning. Said someone killed her. Is that why you're here? Confessing?" he asked with a leer, his gaze dropping to my chest.

I narrowed my eyes at him, realizing he couldn't have been older than twenty. Was this tough guy look all an act?

"Do you have any idea who might've wanted to hurt her? Anyone she'd gotten into a fight with recently?"

"Why should I tell you? Are you with the police?"

"No, I'm just a concerned citizen." That was lame, even to my ears. "I was the one who found her, with Dr. Bennett. Once I heard there was foul play involved, I wanted to try to figure out what happened."

"You found her?" Justin studied me for a moment, then gave a tiny nod, like he was coming to some kind of internal agreement with himself. "Yeah, all right, you can come in. I'll talk to you."

He stepped back from the doorway and held the door open. I hesitated for a moment, then stepped inside. Again, entering the home of a possible killer is not the smartest move, but I wanted to get as much information about Gayle as I could. Plus, this kid was clearly high and didn't look like he could stand up to a punch. I knew I could punch, at least.

Inside, the smell of weed was much stronger. How likely are you to get high from secondhand smoke? I didn't know the answer, but I tried to keep my breaths short to be safe.

The curtains were drawn, which explained the gloom inside. The front door opened up to the living room, where he'd been watching some nature show on the TV. A small kitchen branched off from the living room, and the bedrooms were presumably further down the hallway. I'd make sure not to go back there. I set the flowers down on a small table near the front door.

Justin led me into the living room and plopped down on the couch, picking up a bong and taking a hit. I raised my eyebrows at his actions, but he just blew out a smoke ring, so I turned away and scanned the rest of the room. The terrarium was larger than it had appeared from the doorway, filled with rocks and green plants, but there wasn't anything inside. Maybe a reptile was sleeping under one of the rocks.

"So, what do you want to know? I'm an open book." Justin spread his arms and smiled wide.

"I'm so sorry for your loss. This must be devastating for you."

"I'm getting by."

"I know the police suspect foul play. I wanted to see if you had any idea of who might've wanted to do this to her."

He shrugged. "My mom wasn't Mary Sunshine. Lots of people had their beefs with her."

"Even you?" I winced as the words spilled out of my mouth. Accusing an orphaned kid of murder wasn't high on my list of things I wanted to do today. "Sorry. I just mean...I heard you two got into a fight recently. I'm trying to figure out what happened to her, and I was wondering if you could tell me about it."

His smile dropped. "You're here to accuse me of killing her? Why would I do that?"

"That's not what I said." I glanced around the room. I'd been trying to avoid accusing him of anything, but I still hadn't cracked this slick amateur sleuth persona yet. I was more similar to a Barney Fife character, stumbling onto clues and making a mess of things.

Still, as my gaze landed on a small tin of weed on the

table, I had to wonder if there was a motive here. Maybe Gayle didn't like Justin's little habit and told him to quit, or she'd kick him out of her house. I had to assume he didn't have a job, since he was home at two o'clock on a weekday, and getting kicked out of his house probably wouldn't fare well for him.

"I'm just trying to figure out what happened to her. Can you think of anything that might help me?"

"I don't know why you have all these questions for me. I mean, my mom just died, you know? It's a lot to deal with, man." Suddenly, he burst into tears.

Drat. I'd been trying to avoid something like this. He was clearly going through a lot right now, and someone coming in asking questions like I was would be hard on anyone.

I reached out and patted his arm. "It's all right," I said soothingly, then gasped as he stood and threw his arms around me, beginning to sob into my shirt. Well, at least I could be here for him while he processed his feelings.

As he cried, I continued looking around the rest of the room. It was messy and dark, and it looked like Justin had spread out all his belongings on every surface. Didn't he have any family or friends who could stay with him while he was grieving? I felt bad that he was all alone right now.

I patted Justin's arm as he continued sobbing, though it sounded like he was mostly sniffling now. Could I see this man committing murder? I'd been surprised by a lot of things since coming to Pine Brook. I tried not to make any presumptions about who may or may not be the killer since I was so often wrong. These could've been tears of guilt.

Liam had told me about a fight between the two of them before Gayle's death. Still, a fight between mother and son didn't necessarily lead to murder. I had more than my fair share of fights with my mom growing up. This could've simply been a grieving son.

"Sorry about that." Justin stepped away and wiped his nose with the back of his arm.

"It's all right. I'm sorry for even coming in here like this. I can't imagine what you're going through right now. Can you think of anyone else who might've wanted to kill her?" I asked. "Any enemies?"

Justin went to sit back on the couch, sinking into the cushions. "I don't know. I know she didn't have a lot of friends in town. She spent most of her free time here at home."

"Did she seem upset in the past week or past month? Did she get into any fights with anyone?"

Justin shook his head, wiping his nose with his arm. "She didn't really tell me much about that."

I deflated and looked around the rest of the room. I'd been hoping that Justin would have some hint as to what had happened to his mother, but it sounded like he was as much in the dark about it as I was.

"You know who you should talk to?" he asked, and my head shot up at his words. "Deborah Li. At the clinic? She hated my mom."

"Really?" I asked, raising my eyebrows. I'd briefly seen Deborah and Gayle interacting in the hallway of the clinic, and their relationship had seemed tense. Was there something more sinister going on between them?

"Yeah." Justin nodded, his head bobbing as he got into the rhythm of the story. "Mom talked about it all the time. She said that Dr. Li always thought she was better than everyone else, and my mom could tell. She didn't want to put up with it. Maybe she finally stood up to her, so Dr. Li killed her."

As far as motives went, it wasn't the best I'd seen, but it was something. No one at the clinic had mentioned anything about Deborah and Gayle not getting along, though. Were people keeping things from me?

Suddenly, something slid over my foot, thick and long and hard. I jumped into the air with a shriek. A giant snake slithered across the floor, its forked tongue flicking out at me.

I SCURRIED AWAY from the snake, bumping into the coffee table and knocking over Justin's bong. The snake was red and brown striped, about as wide as a water bottle and several feet long.

"Hey, be careful!" Justin said, shooting up from his seat and steadying the bong. "You're scaring Priscilla."

"Priscilla?" I was crammed into the corner of the living room as far from the snake as I could get.

"Come here, Priscilla." Justin cooed as he approached the snake. He lifted the snake off the floor and draped it over his shoulders. "You shouldn't scream. You'll scare her."

"Why do you have a snake?" I asked, my heart rate finally returning to normal.

Justin shrugged as he slipped the snake back into the terrarium. "I just like them. They're pretty cool." He stared through the glass, watching Priscilla, and I could've sworn I saw his tongue dart out, like a snake's. That might've just been my imagination. I hoped it was.

"Your mom let you keep a snake here?" I asked, stepping away from the wall and back to the front door, giving the snake a wide berth.

"She wasn't around much because of work. She wanted

me to get a dog, so I wouldn't be home alone all the time, but I preferred a snake." He patted the terrarium, grinning widely. "I've had Priscilla here for six years."

"How nice," I murmured, checking to make sure I had my purse and jacket. I was done talking to snake boy.

"Well, thanks for your time," I said. "I am sorry about your mom. If you think of anything else important, you can find me at the Hemlock Inn."

"Do you want to stay?" Justin asked suddenly, taking a step closer to me in front of the doorway. "We could watch TV or something," he added, gesturing to the screen, which had been playing an Animal Planet show. At least the kid was consistent about his interests.

"I really need to get back to work," I said, stepping around him and closer to the front door. I felt bad for the kid, but I didn't want to hang out with a snake. "Could you call a friend, someone to hang out so you have some company?"

"Yeah, I guess I could do that," he mumbled. "Nice to meet you."

"You too. If you think of anything else that might be helpful, you should reach out to the police," I added.

"Nah, man, I don't want to talk to the police," he said, crossing his arms sullenly.

"Why not?"

He spread his arms out, gesturing to the weed paraphernalia on the table. Ah, yes, of course.

"I thought weed was legal in Washington?"

"Even still, man, I don't want anyone sniffing around too closely. They could suddenly change the rules on us again, and then I'd be out of luck."

Plus, there were all those run-ins with the police Patel

had mentioned yesterday. It looked like there were several reasons for Justin to stay away from the police.

He didn't say anything else, so I took that as my cue to leave, practically running through the front door and shutting it behind me. A chill raced through me as I remembered the feeling of Priscilla slithering over my foot, and I hurried back to my car to get away from the two of them. Visiting with snakes was not high on my list of things to do today. I climbed into my car and peeled away from the curb, heading back to the inn.

As I drove, I thought over all I'd learned from Justin. I didn't think he was a killer—he might've gotten angry sometimes, but it was probably more like a toddler having a temper tantrum. He didn't seem likely to plan out a multi-step murder involving stealing pills from someone in town and slipping them into his mother's coffee.

Justin wasn't a model citizen, but he didn't seem like a murderer to me. Back to square one.

12

I stopped off at the inn, wondering if I needed a shower after that visit with Justin and Priscilla. I didn't think I smelled like weed, but it was hard to tell on my own. I'd been gone from the inn for a while and wanted to make sure everything was okay. Now, with Estelle at risk of getting arrested, and with Gayle's murdered body imprinted in my brain, I'd gotten swept up in another murder investigation keeping me from the inn. My priorities were all out of whack.

Still, I felt pretty icky after talking to Justin, and not just because of the smell of weed now stuck to my clothes. I was sticking my nose into something that didn't concern me, and I'd already been told by the police once to stay out of this case. As much as I wanted to help my friend, it was probably best to leave the investigation to the police.

I parked my car at the inn and hurried inside to the lobby. Nadia was at the front desk, and I headed over to her to see if she needed any help.

"Oh, god, you smell like weed," she said, scrunching her

nose as I approached the front desk. Drat. I guess it was pretty strong.

"Sorry," I said, keeping my distance from the desk. Fortunately, there weren't any guests in the lobby to hear her. "I was just visiting someone whose place smelled."

"Making friends with potheads?" Nadia asked with a smirk.

"Not exactly," I said. "Do you need me up here? If not, I'm going to take a shower."

"Yes, that seems like a good idea for the sake of everyone's noses."

I jokingly stuck my tongue out at her, then headed to the spare shower we kept onsite for inn employees. As I crossed the lobby, a woman walked through the front door of the inn. She was tall, with thick blonde hair that curled down her back in waves, a round—practically cherubic—face, and an artistically placed mole on her cheek. I slowed as she approached, not wanting to be rude to a guest but hoping she wouldn't get close enough to smell the weed.

"Good afternoon," I said, smiling as she approached. "Checking in?" She didn't have any bags with her, but that wasn't totally strange. She may have left them in her car or only needed the items she could fit in her tiny purse.

"No, I'm actually looking for someone," she said, coming to stand near me. Her nose crinkled as she approached, undoubtedly picking up the scent of Justin's weed, but she didn't say anything.

"Well, maybe we can help," I said, taking a tiny step backwards. She'd get used to the smell eventually, right? "Who are you looking for?"

"Nick, the produce guy? I'm his girlfriend."

～

I DIDN'T EXACTLY REMEMBER HELPING this woman. I knew that I somehow got her over to Nadia at the front desk, who was able to convey to her that Nick wasn't around right now, but that we'd let her know as soon as we heard from him. I figured the best use of my time was sitting on the couch in front of the unlit fireplace, staring into the ash.

Nick had a girlfriend? He'd never told me about her. Of course, he didn't have to tell me about everything going on in his life, but I'd had the impression that he was single and that he liked me. But now that I thought about it, he never did say, one way or the other, if he was actually single.

"Are you okay?" Nadia stood in front of me, her arms crossed, looking uncomfortable.

I'd put my head between my legs to try to stop any dizziness, but that must've looked pretty strange to someone else. The other woman had left the lobby at some point.

"Is she gone?" I blurted out before I had a chance to think.

Nadia nodded slowly. "Yes. I told her Nick wasn't here, but that we'd let her know if he comes by. She doesn't check out until later this week, so they'll probably run into each other."

"She's staying here?!" My words came out in a shout, and Nadia's eyes widened at my outburst.

"Yes. Is there a problem?"

I shook my head, not trusting what I would say if I opened my mouth. Nick, who'd just invited me to his apartment for dinner, had a girlfriend who was now staying at my inn. What else could possibly go wrong?

"*Are* you okay?" Nadia asked again. "You look kind of...weird."

That was an understatement, but I didn't correct her. "I'm fine," I said instead, standing up and walking away from the couch. "Just tired, is all. Listen, I've got some work to do in the back office. Will you be okay up here?" I knew I kept asking Nadia if she could handle running the front desk alone, and clearly she could, but my thoughts were all scattered right now.

"Sure thing," she said, heading back to the front desk. "Maybe drink some water, though. You look kind of...sickly."

As I headed to my office, I couldn't get that woman's face out of my mind. Why had Nick lied to me? I suppose he wasn't obligated to tell me about a girlfriend, but he'd definitely omitted that important information, especially after agreeing to go on a date with me. Was it possible I misunderstood the situation? Maybe the woman had meant *girlfriend* in some other way?

That didn't make any sense, even I could see that. The smart thing to do was talk to Nick and ask him what was going on, but my pride wouldn't let me. I'd been hurt before by a lying cheater, and I wasn't interested in playing more games.

I went back to the office, where I knew I could get some peace and quiet. Settling myself into the leather chair behind the desk, I switched on the computer and pulled up the inn's financial statements. I needed to balance the books and check that we were spending money responsibly. I didn't know how long Tracy would be gone for, and I couldn't let this work fall to the wayside while she was gone.

Instead, the numbers swam in front of my eyes as that woman's face kept popping into my head. It hurt to know that Nick had lied to me, and I couldn't stop thinking about it.

I took a deep breath and sighed out my exhale, pulling up Facebook. I'd decided to stop snooping around Gayle's life after seeing how upset Justin was about her death, but I couldn't focus right now and needed to do something with my thoughts. Gayle had to have a Facebook, right? Maybe I could learn something about what had happened to her there.

Ten minutes later, I sat back in the chair, stumped. "Gayle Hart" was a pretty common name, and even filtering by location down to Washington hadn't given me any good leads. Was it possible she wasn't on Facebook? I should've asked Justin to show me her social media pages before I left their house, but I wasn't interested in spending any more time with Priscilla than I had to.

Putting the computer back to sleep, I pulled out a notepad and pen from the drawer. If social media wasn't getting me anywhere, I'd at least try to be methodical about my investigation. I didn't want to run around town following leads given to me by potential suspects, which is what I'd been doing with Justin. Who's to say that Liam was telling the truth about Justin's relationship with his mom? Better to lay out all I knew and see what jumped out at me.

At the top of the page, I wrote *Suspects*, underlined it, then started a list down below. Both doctors went to the top, followed by Justin. Maria had acted strange at the clinic, so I added her name to the list. I moved down to the bottom of the page and wrote Estelle's name in tiny letters. I didn't actually think she was a murderer, but she was involved in all this if her pills were used. Did the killer know about their tense relationship and used it to their advantage?

Justin had mentioned that Deborah and his mom hated each other, so I underlined the doctor's name. She hadn't been at the clinic when I'd stopped by earlier, at least not that I'd seen. She must've lived in town, though. Could I get her address from someone?

Below the names, I wrote *Time of death* with a big question mark next to it. I could have as many suspects on my list as I wanted, but what I needed to do was check alibis. However, I didn't know when Gayle was exposed to the pills, or how long it took them for them to kill her. She'd died in the morning, so when did the pills end up in her system? How did the killer get them into her system?

I sat back and stared at my list. Not very long. Maybe I should talk to Patel and see what she'd learned so far. The detective tried to avoid sharing too much information about active cases with me since I was a civilian, but she'd been known to drop a clue or two in the past.

My phone buzzed in my pocket, and I pulled it out and read a text from Miles.

Estelle and I are home now. Ron was able to talk to the detective. We'll talk soon.

Good to know that Miles and Ron were able to bring Estelle home after her visit with the police. It seemed they didn't have enough to arrest her, at least not right now.

I stood and stuck the notepad in one of the drawers. My mind was still buzzing from all these suspects and questions, but I wanted to check on my friend.

13

E stelle and Miles lived just off the main street of town. I wanted to know what the police had told them, which would hopefully distract me from whatever was going on with Nick.

Ron answered the door at the Adlers' home. "Come in, come in," he said, motioning me into the house and hurriedly shutting the door behind us.

"What are you doing here?" I asked, slipping off my coat and hanging it up on the rack by the door.

Ron sighed, kneading his hands together. Beads of sweat had appeared along his forehead. "Miles asked me to stay. He's worried about Estelle and didn't know what she'd do if I left."

I raised my eyebrows. "He thinks she might hurt herself?" I'd never known Estelle to respond to tough situations in that manner.

"Oh, goodness, no, no," Ron said quickly. "Nothing like that! He's afraid Estelle will run off and try to find the killer. She's quite upset about all this business with the police and believes that the only thing to do is to find the real culprit."

I had to smile at that. That sounded exactly like the Estelle I knew. Not content to sit around and wait for the police to do their jobs, she would rush right off and try to figure it out herself. Especially if she thought the police were going after the wrong person.

"I think I'll be able to calm her down," I said to Ron. "I've been doing some snooping around myself, and I've got some potential suspects. That's why I came over here. I'll make sure she doesn't leave."

"Oh, thank you," Ron said, surprising me with a hug. "I need to get back to my office. I've got another client coming in shortly, and I didn't know when I'd get a chance to leave." He grabbed a coat from the coat rack and turned back to the front door. "Will you let them know I had to scurry?" he said to me over his shoulder as he rushed out the door.

I turned back to the Adlers' home. The front door led off directly to the living room, which was currently empty. Two bedrooms and bathrooms were in the back of the house. You had to pass by the kitchen first to get to them, and that's where I found Miles and Estelle. Estelle was seated at the counter on a stool, and Miles was bustling around her, refilling her tea and setting out a plate of cookies. I could hear them arguing from the living room.

"You heard Ron. You can't go anywhere right now," Miles said.

"Someone needs to find the real killer," Estelle responded. "I don't care what the police say or what Ron thinks. I didn't do this, and if I don't get at the truth, who knows what the police might do next!"

"If you go back out there, you'll just make the police think you're even more guilty. I can't lose you."

"He's right," I said, stepping into the kitchen. "The best thing you can do right now is stay here."

"Oh, Simone!" Estelle cried out at my entrance. She hopped off her stool and rushed over to me, pulling me into a tight hug. I returned the hug and glanced over her shoulder at Miles, who was grinning from ear to ear.

"Ron had to get back to his office, but I told him I'd check on you two," I said. Estelle and I went back to the stool she'd been sitting at, and Miles set down a mug for me.

"Well, thank you for stopping by," Estelle said. She rubbed the back of her neck and yawned. She looked like she'd aged a few years since I last saw her.

"What did the police say to you? Patel mentioned that they found your pill bottle at the crime scene. She thought your pills were involved."

Estelle nodded. "Yes, they told me that, too. I told her I lost them but I'm not sure if she believed me. It's not a secret that I take those pills, or that Gayle was allergic to soy, and it wouldn't have been hard for someone to take them from my purse. I'm sure I've left my purse sitting out at the bistro while I used the restroom. Anyone could have grabbed them. I told the police all of this, but they're so cagey with their information. I even asked Miriam what she knew, but she said she couldn't talk to me."

"Did they ask about an alibi?" If I could figure out Gayle's time of death, I would have a better shot at narrowing down which suspects had the opportunity to slip her the pills.

To my surprise, Estelle shook her head. "I thought they would ask about that, and I thought I'd be out of luck since I was home alone when you found Gayle's body." She reached over and squeezed Miles' hand. "This guy was out playing cards with his friends." She turned back to me. "But they didn't ask about that. I got the sense they didn't know exactly when it happened."

That was strange. True, you couldn't directly pinpoint every death to a specific time, but since Gayle had died in the morning, she'd probably been exposed to the pills within an hour or two of dying. I made a mental note to ask Patel about that as soon as I could.

"Enough about my horrid trip to the police. Can you please explain to Miles that someone needs to find the real killer before the police throw me in jail?"

"I agree that the police are probably too focused on you right now and may need some help with finding the actual killer"—Estelle began cheering at my words, so I quickly hurried on— "but I don't think you are the right person to do that. If the police see you running around, snooping, they're likely to think you're just trying to get in the way and frame someone else for what you did."

Estelle opened her mouth, undoubtedly to interrupt with some kind of argument, so I quickly hurried on. "Lucky for you, your best friend has found one or two killers in the past, and is already looking into Gayle's death."

Estelle cheered at my words, and Miles looked very relieved. "So, what have you found out?" Estelle asked, leaning forward in her seat.

I took them through Maria's strange reaction to my questions, speaking with Liam and learning about Justin, all the suspicions I had about Justin, and the way he pointed me towards Deborah.

"I haven't gotten ahold of Deborah just yet, but that will be my next step. Honestly, I can see all of them playing some role in Gayle's death. It's too early to say for sure what happened."

Estelle gasped. "Not Liam, right? He's too kind to have killed Gayle."

I hesitated. I had a feeling Liam's good looks were skewing Estelle's perception of him. He had seemed very kind when I spoke with him, but it wasn't impossible to cover up that kind of thing. I couldn't let his attractiveness and kindness blind me from the truth.

"We shouldn't assume anyone is incapable of murder," I said. "Given all the murderers we've seen in this town, it would be presumptuous to think that anyone in the victim's life isn't a suspect. Half the time, we're completely surprised by the truth."

"I suppose you're right." Estelle took a sip of her tea and tilted her head to the side, thinking. "Based on everyone you've spoken with so far, who do you think is the killer?"

"I'm not sure. Like I said, I think it's too early to say definitively one way or the other. Everyone in Gayle's life needs to be looked at closely." I took a deep breath to prepare for what I was about to say next. "Including, unfortunately, you."

Estelle reared back in her seat like I'd slapped her, and Miles gasped. "You can't really believe she had anything to do with it, can you?" he asked.

"I don't believe you're a killer," I said, reaching out and squeezing Estelle's hand. "But the police brought you in for a reason. Maybe you know something that might point to the truth. What was really going on between you and Gayle? Why did you two hate each other so much?"

Estelle sighed and stared down into her mug, then looked up at me and cracked a smile. "I guess it's probably best to get this all out there. It'll come out eventually, won't it? Gayle and I became friends when Miles and I first moved to Pine Brook. He and I were looking for someplace to settle down, and this town is so charming. We didn't know many people, but everyone we met was kind.

"I had an infection when we first got to town, and I had to go to the clinic a lot in the early days. Gayle was the only nurse at the time, so we spent a lot of time talking to each other. I thought she was abrasive at first, but she had a great sense of humor. We ended up bonding over our love of baking."

I leaned back in my seat but tried to keep my face neutral. Estelle had made it seem like she and Gayle barely knew each other, yet they'd apparently had a close relationship at one point in time. What had happened to cause a rift between them? I couldn't imagine what Estelle was going through right now, knowing that she'd lost someone she'd once been close to. And had been accused of her murder!

"Justin was a teenager at the time, and he was constantly acting out. Gayle would talk about how hard it was raising him on her own. His father ran out when he was a baby, and it was just the two of them for so long. She did the best she could, but it was still hard." Estelle paused again, taking a shaky breath.

Miles reached out and squeezed her hand. "It's all right," he said, his voice low. "You can tell her."

Estelle nodded and looked up at me, straight into my eyes. "She spent a lot of time complaining about all the trouble Justin was getting into, and how no one understood how hard it was to take care of him. One day, we got into an argument. I told her I thought she was being too lenient with Justin, and that was why he was acting out. She...didn't take it well. We both said some things we later regretted, but the damage was done. We stopped talking after that fight. Now that she's gone, I wish...I wish we'd talked things through."

Estelle sat back in her seat, cradling her head in her hands as the words left her body. I reached over and squeezed her arm while Miles gave her a hug.

"You couldn't have known what would happen," I said. "She should've let you talk to her and explain. People say things they don't mean all the time. She shouldn't have pushed you away like that."

Estelle looked up at me, a creaky smile on her face. "Thanks, I appreciate the support, but you're wrong. I was a bad friend. It's as simple as that. I agree that Gayle let it fester for too long, and we probably should've made up years ago, but I did something awful that day. I'm so ashamed to even think about it."

I turned over what she said in my head, thinking. "Okay, so you two had a falling out a few years ago and stopped being friends. Why would the police think that means you killed her? It sounds like she had a better reason to want to harm you, instead."

Miles jumped in. "That's the question I have. I asked the police that, but they didn't say much. Since Estelle's pills ultimately killed Gayle, when they uncovered this past that Estelle hadn't mentioned, they got suspicious. They said maybe Gayle came to Estelle and taunted her more than Estelle could handle since that was something that Gayle would do, and Estelle snapped. She saw an opportunity to get rid of someone who argued with her every chance she got, and she took it. At least, that's what the police seem to think. It's not a very good argument, in my opinion, but the police are looking for any proof they can find."

"But how would you have known that Gayle was allergic to soy and that she'd have an allergic reaction to your pills?"

"Oh, everyone knew Gayle had that allergy," Estelle said. "She was always complaining about all the foods she couldn't eat and how much harder life was for her because of it. She'd tell anyone who would listen about this allergy. If you decided you wanted to kill her, all you'd need to do was look up the allergy and see what might cause an allergic reaction."

Gayle had blown up at Stella at the coffee shop over suspected soy milk in her coffee. Anyone in a five-mile radius would've known that Gayle couldn't eat soy after that.

"Well, how would they know what you took? We have to assume that the killer stole your pills," I said. "Let's say they did look up what would cause an allergic reaction in Gayle and figured they could slip the pills into something she ate, as I can't imagine someone force-feeding her the pills. How would the killer know that you took soy supplements?"

Estelle shrugged. "I'm not shy about sharing what I take, either. I mean, I don't go around blabbing it to everyone in town, but I pick them up at the pharmacy in town, and I'm sure I've mentioned to people how much they help with my hot flashes. I've probably told a lot of people about them. Now I know I should keep that kind of thing quiet."

It was a stretch, but it was possible someone had known that Estelle had taken these supplements and what they would do to Gayle if they were introduced into her system. Gayle's employers probably knew about her allergy, but, more than likely, so did her son. The way Gayle had yelled about her allergy at Cuppa Joe's earlier in the week meant everyone in town probably knew, too. I couldn't cross anyone off my list yet. This case was going to be a tough one to solve.

"All right, you two should stay here." I stood and carried my mug over to the sink. "I don't want Patel to get any ideas about us snooping around. If she knows you're asking questions, she might look at you more suspiciously."

Estelle nodded while Miles took over washing up my mug. "What are you going to do?" he asked.

"Well, I'm still going to ask questions. I'll try to keep quiet about it, but I can't just sit around while the police build a case against you. I know you didn't do this, so now it's just time to find someone else who could've."

"Oh, thank you!" Estelle hopped out of her seat and pulled me into a bone-crushing hug. When she was excited, the woman was strong. I patted her on the back, trying to hold in my reaction to the pain.

"I'll call you if I find out anything important." I gave Miles a quick hug, then left their home.

Outside, night had fallen. The air was cold and crisp, and my breath fogged in front of my face. I shoved my hands into my pockets to keep them warm, then hurried to my car.

Was I really getting involved in another murder investigation? Why did this town even have so much murder? These were important questions to consider, but I was bone-tired and just wanted to go home and sleep. Before I did that, there was someone I wanted to talk to who might be able to talk some sense into me. Or yell at me; it was always hard to say.

14

"The police are going to start thinking you're killing everyone in town for kicks. Have you thought of that?"

I rolled my eyes at my sister's histrionics. She wasn't yelling, but I wasn't getting talked out of anything, either.

"This is Estelle; you know I can't just let this go," I said, slipping off Lola's harness and giving the dog a treat.

I'd gotten back to my apartment after meeting with the Adlers and had taken Lola out for a walk around the block so she could do her business. She was now trotting back to the bedroom, where I knew she would spin around three times on the bed, then collapse down and fall asleep immediately.

I'd called Chrissy as we were heading back, hoping I could catch her before she went to bed. She was just down in L.A. but it was much later than I had realized, and I didn't know if she'd already be asleep. Fortunately, my older sister was a night owl and always available for a phone call.

"I know you have this desire to help your friends, but one day it's going to get you into a lot of trouble," Chrissy said. "I'd just hate to see the police suspect you of something because you snuck into the dead woman's house."

"This dead woman lived with her son, so I was welcomed right into their house," I said. "I haven't done anything illegal." *Yet*, I added to myself.

"Yet," Chrissy said, reading my mind. I held in a groan. "I know how much you care about Estelle. I just don't want to see you get hurt."

I noticed Chrissy didn't seem to have these issues with me snooping around when she'd been the one suspected of murder. I kept that thought to myself, though. I wasn't interested in getting into an actual argument with her this late in the day.

"Look, I just thought I should let you know what was going on and see if you had any advice," I said, flipping off the lights in the living room and padding across the hardwood floor to my bedroom. "I'm not looking for a lecture."

Chrissy sighed, and the sound of rustling came across the line. "I know," she said, her voice now muffled.

I paused and cocked my head at the sound. "Are you eating a snack? While I'm discussing a murder investigation?"

"Hey, you're the one who called me at midnight," she said, now not disguising the sound of a chip bag. "I can't help it if your antics make me hungry."

I laughed, putting my phone on speakerphone and changing into pajamas. "No, I guess you're right. I'm sorry for calling so late. I just needed to talk to someone."

"Don't worry about it. I was already up." Of course she was! And yet, she was trying to make me feel bad about calling. "So, what's your plan with all of this? If you know Estelle didn't do it, who do you think did?"

I chewed the inside of my cheek, thinking. "I've been

talking to the people Gayle worked with, but honestly, she was such an odious woman, I could see many people deciding they wanted to kill her. Her son was pretty odd, though I should cut him some slack since he's grieving. He did turn their entire house into a giant bong, though. I'm pretty sure I got a contact high just from standing in his living room."

Chrissy laughed at that.

"I can't imagine that Gayle the nurse would've let him smoke so much while she was alive," I said, going into the bathroom with the phone and starting my nightly routine of tooth brushing and face washing. "Now that she's gone, he doesn't need to hide his illegal activities."

"Isn't marijuana legal in Washington state?" Chrissy chimed in.

I paused and looked up at the mirror over the sink, thinking. "You're right, but I'm not totally sure if all of his weed is legal. Honestly, I can't keep up with all these laws."

Chrissy laughed. "No, there are so many of them to keep up with. Okay, so her son might've wanted to get rid of mommy dearest so he could light up every night. That's hardly a motive. Who else? You say she was a nurse? What about the doctors she worked with? I imagine they would know exactly which pills would cause an allergic reaction in her, and they'd know which pills Estelle was taking, right?"

"That's what I'm thinking," I said, finishing up by patting moisturizer on my cheeks. I flipped off the bathroom light and went back into the bedroom. "Today, I talked with one of the doctors, who did seem pretty distraught over Gayle's death. He'd told me before she died that he kept her employed even though he knew she was abrasive because kids loved her and most of the patients warmed up to her. But he might've been lying straight to my face."

"What about the other doctor? You said she worked with more than one?"

"Yes, there's one more doctor at the clinic. Actually, Gayle's son said I should talk to her next. Apparently, he didn't like her very much, and he claims neither did his mother. I want to talk to her myself, of course. She may have a more obvious motive than the other doctor if it was known that they hated each other. Maybe something set her off."

"You've got to wonder what made this happen now, you know?" Chrissy said. "People don't suddenly decide to murder. Did something big happen, and the killer finally realized they couldn't handle her anymore? Did Gayle learn something she wasn't supposed to? There's a secret out there that someone would kill to keep that way."

Chrissy was right. The murderer wouldn't have just stumbled into killing Gayle in this way. The manner of death made me think that they'd been planning this for a while. They had to sneak away Estelle's pills, then give them to Gayle without her noticing. That took planning and ingenuity.

Did Justin seem like the kind of person who could pull off something like that? He did have the most access to his mother, but how easily could he get Estelle's pills? If I knew what time Gayle had been given the pills, I could more easily look at alibis and figure out who would've had the opportunity to do it. Means and opportunity were only part of it, of course. What was Justin's motive? How did he really feel about his mother?

"Please be careful," Chrissy said, pulling me out of my thoughts. "I know you can't seem to stay away from these murder investigations, so I won't tell you to do that, but try not to do anything extra dangerous, okay?"

"I promise," I said, smiling. She couldn't help but look

out for me. "Listen, I have to go, but thanks for talking. I'll let you know if anything changes."

"Yes, let me know if Estelle needs help with a lawyer. I'm sure Mark knows someone up there who could help." Chrissy's husband did contract law, but apparently knew lawyers up and down the West Coast. He'd offered his help on more than one occasion, and, one day, I was probably going to need his assistance.

We said our goodbyes, and I hung up the phone. Tossing it onto my nightstand, I flopped back onto my bed, staring up at the ceiling. Gayle's face ran through my head as if asking me to find her killer. Chrissy was right to warn me to be careful; I couldn't underestimate a killer, especially one who had spent so much time planning to murder Gayle. Who knows what they might do if they felt threatened?

I FELL ASLEEP SOON after that and slept like a log through the night. I woke up before my alarm in the morning and changed into running clothes. The sun hadn't risen fully, but I could see it begin to peek over the horizon as I laced up my running shoes and looked out the front window to check the weather.

As I ran through my neighborhood, my feet pounding against the pavement, the sun continued to rise, and by the time I returned to my apartment after a three-mile loop, it was hanging lazily in the sky, and my mind felt clear. I'd had a little back pain at the beginning of the run, but it had actually improved by the time I was done.

My first stop today was to talk to Dr. Deborah Li. After what Justin had told me about her feelings about his mom, I needed to learn more about her. She'd seemed aloof and efficient when I saw her briefly at the clinic, but Liam was willing to go into business with her, so maybe there was more to her than I had seen. Of course, they had also dated briefly, so maybe that was why opening the clinic together had seemed like a good idea. The only way I was going to find out was if I asked.

Back in my apartment, I showered and changed into jeans and a sweater. Though the sun was out, it was still chilly outside, so I grabbed a jacket and boots as I left. It was still early enough that I could justify not stopping off at the inn right away. Nadia would show up for her shift in an hour, and there weren't likely to be any guests needing help until then.

What I wanted to do was talk to Tracy, but she was currently unavailable while she dealt with her family issue. She never talked about her family much—when Chrissy was visiting last year, she'd told me she had sisters—but I knew she wouldn't leave the inn so suddenly like this without a good reason.

We still hadn't had a chance to talk about that woman who'd shown up at the inn—whom I'd spilled soapy water on, I remembered with a cringe—and I didn't know when we'd get a chance to now that Tracy was out of town dealing with something else.

Down in the apartment lobby, the building was quiet. Nick came through the front door right as I hit the last step. I tried to climb back up the stairs before he could see me, but I was too slow.

"Good morning, Simone!" he said, strolling over to me. He was wearing jeans and a navy blue flannel over a white t-shirt. In his arms, he carried a box stuffed with asparagus.

"Morning," I said, squeezing past him in the lobby. My pride was still stinging from running into his supposed girl-friend at the inn. I probably should've given him the benefit of the doubt and asked about her, but I'd already been so open and honest about my feelings with him. I wasn't willing to face the truth.

"Would you like any of these?" He stepped in front of me to block my way and held out the box of asparagus. "I dropped off deliveries to all my customers, and we had extra. I was gonna try to grill them up later, but even this is too many for me!"

The box was overflowing with green stalks. "You have a grill?" I asked. My instinct was to dash out of here as fast as I could, but a part of me couldn't help but engage with him. How did he have a grill in his tiny apartment? The units in this building didn't have outdoor space.

"Oh, you haven't seen the grill? It's on the roof," Nick explained. "I'm surprised I haven't taken you up there yet. It's still pretty chilly for true grilling, but when the sun is out, you gotta take advantage of it when you can. Maybe I can grill for us on Friday."

"Oh, maybe," I said, sliding past him. "You should probably grill for your girlfriend instead of me. I have to go now," I added, hustling out of the lobby, my cheeks burning.

Why did I have to bring up his girlfriend? Maybe that was one of those things that we just didn't talk about? I didn't wait to hear what he had to say. I just needed to get out of there.

I peeled out of the parking lot as soon as I got into my car, not looking back at Nick. He wasn't likely to lie to me, he'd been honest with me from the second I'd met him, so it was very possible that I'd misunderstood the situation with this woman at the inn. Maybe they'd had a bad breakup, and she couldn't admit to others that they were over? Or maybe he was the kind of guy who tried to have his cake and eat it, too.

There were a million explanations for what was really going on, but I was too embarrassed to wait around and hear them. It hurt to learn about his girlfriend after asking him out on a date, and I was having trouble getting past those feelings. Still, I was being too cold with him. I'd have to talk to him eventually. Right now, though, I had a killer to catch.

15

I didn't know exactly where to start to find Dr. Li, but I knew I needed coffee to get my day going. I parked outside of Cuppa Joe's and hurried inside, putting in my order at the front. The coffee shop was quiet this morning, and I chatted with one of the baristas while I waited for my drink.

"Pretty crazy what happened to Gayle," he said, wiping down the counter between us. His light brown skin was more flawless than mine, and he had a diamond stud in his left ear.

"Pretty sad, too. I feel bad for her son." I leaned my hip against the countertop.

"I heard the police think it was murder," the barista said, leaning in and lowering his voice a notch. "Someone killed her to keep their secret."

Suddenly, a plate crashed to the ground behind the counter. We both looked up and saw Stella standing a couple feet away, her hands still in the air from when she'd dropped the plate, her eyes wide and terrified.

"Sorry about that," she muttered, turning on her heel and going through the door to the back of the coffee shop.

"What was that about?" I asked as the barista handed me my coffee.

"No idea." He shrugged. "She's been acting weird all week. Enjoy your drink!"

I waved goodbye and left the coffee shop, taking a sip as I left. What had spooked Stella? Was she sick or something? Or had she overheard us talking about Gayle? She might've just been tired. No reason to go around assuming everyone is a suspect when I didn't have any proof.

Once my coffee was in hand, I sat in my car and thought about where to go next. I didn't know exactly where to start, but my best bet for finding Dr. Li was to go back to the last —and only—place I'd seen her: the clinic.

The lot was full when I pulled up to the building, but I snagged a spot near the front as someone was leaving. Heading inside, I could hear chatter from the waiting room before I got down the hallway.

All the seats in the waiting room were full. A woman, not Maria, sat behind the front desk, talking to a patient. A long line spun out from behind the first person at the front desk. Why were there so many people here? Was there some kind of sickness going around that I didn't know about?

My name was called from the crowd, and I looked around, spotting a woman sitting in one of the plastic chairs and waving to me from across the waiting room. She was about eighty years old, named Kathleen, and she'd helped me out with an investigation a few months ago. We'd seen each other around town since then, always stopping to chat whenever we had time. Maybe she could explain what was going on here.

"It's so nice to see you," I said, slipping into the one open seat next to Kathleen. "I can't believe the lobby is so crowded. Is there some bug going around?"

"I hope not. I'm just here to get my flu shot, but I was told I'd have to wait thirty minutes. Luckily I brought something to keep me busy." She held up knitting needles and a scarf she was working on.

"Where's Maria? I don't recognize the woman at the front desk."

"That's what I asked, too," Kathleen said. "Apparently, Maria didn't show up for work today, so Dr. Bennett had to call in some extra help. And now, with Gayle gone, it seems like they are really backed up here."

Where was Maria? She'd run off when I'd asked her questions the day before; had she run out of town because she was involved in Gayle's death?

"Is Dr. Li here?" I asked Kathleen.

She shook her head. "No, Dr. Bennett is all alone today. Every time he comes into the waiting room to take the next patient, he looks more and more worn down. Poor man."

Had Dr. Li skipped work because she was guilty too? Why was everyone abandoning this clinic?

"Any idea where Dr. Li is?" I asked. "I was hoping to talk to her about something."

"I'm not so sure. Dr. Bennett isn't saying anything, and that poor girl at the front desk seems extremely lost. I don't know if Dr. Li is sick, or out of town, or what."

This was going to make it very difficult for me to question Dr. Li about her involvement in Gayle's death and the claims Justin had made against her. However, if she had fled town, that would probably give the police a strong reason to go after her. Why would she leave so suddenly after Gayle's death?

"Are you here about Gayle?" Kathleen asked, and I looked over at her sharply. Had she read my mind?

When I didn't say anything right away, Kathleen went on, continuing to knit. "It's dreadful to hear about her death. I mean, I didn't like the woman very much, either, but she didn't deserve to die. I heard the police brought Estelle in for questioning. I can't believe she had anything to do with it, but I know the police are just trying to get to the truth. Is that why you're here? Because you think Estelle is innocent?"

I nodded. There was no use trying to keep anything from this astute geriatric. "I wanted to talk to Dr. Li to see if she had any idea about who might've killed Gayle. But if she's not here, I'm not really sure where to go next." If the doctor had fled town after the murder, she could've been anywhere by now.

"You should try her home," Kathleen said. "Maybe her husband knows where she is. I normally wouldn't go knocking on my doctor's door, but I agree that it seems very strange for her to be gone right now. Plus, I feel bad for Dr. Bennett. Dr. Li should be here helping him."

"This is amazing information. Do you know where she lives?"

"Sure. It's the big red house on Clancy Street. You can't miss it."

"Thanks! Good luck with your flu shot." I stood up to leave, the waiting room still as packed as it had been when I'd first shown up.

I let out a sigh of relief as I left the building. Sitting in a room full of sick people for much longer was not high on my list of things to do. I finished my coffee in my car and headed towards Clancy Street.

I knew I was probably needed at the inn, especially with

Tracy gone, but all I could think about while at the inn was Nick's girlfriend staying in one of the rooms. Talking to Dr. Li would help keep my mind off things.

Dr. Li's home was in a nice part of town, not far from the clinic, on a street lined with tall oak trees and manicured lawns. All the homes were set back far from the street, and each probably had large backyards, too. Her home was a large Victorian, freshly painted, with rose bushes lining the walkway up to the porch.

All the plants were beautifully maintained; how much free time did she have to care for her plants? Or did she hire professionals to come in and care for them? Given the size of the house and the rest of the houses on the block, I had a feeling her work at the clinic brought in enough income each month to justify a gardener.

I rang the doorbell and waited for a response. Dark clouds were gathering to the east; a storm was headed our way. I tapped my foot as I waited for someone to answer the door, impatient, not interested in getting stuck outside in the rain.

Dr. Li answered the door, wearing black slacks and a cashmere sweater that looked more expensive than my car payment. Her feet were bare, and her hair was pulled up into a high bun, tendrils of dark hair hanging loose across her face. Her eyes were blank when she saw me, though she squinted as she tried to recognize me.

"Hi, Dr. Li, sorry to bother you," I said. "I'm Simone. I was just at the clinic a few days ago. Dr. Bennett examined me. I, um, found Gayle's body with him."

Realization dawned on her face, though she didn't warm up to me. "Oh, yes, that's right. I recognize you from around town. What are you doing here?"

"I was hoping I could talk with you. I went to the clinic

first, but since you weren't there, someone told me where you lived. I'm trying to get to the bottom of what happened to Gayle, and I wanted to ask you a few questions."

Her face closed off at that, and she started closing the door. "The police have already been by. You should leave this to them. I have nothing to say to you."

"I know the police have already spoken with you," I said, slipping my foot into the doorway before she could shut it, catching the door on my shoe. Thank goodness I'd worn boots today! Dr. Li snapped her gaze up to me, her eyes narrowed.

"I just have a few questions. It won't take long," I went on. "I spoke with Gayle's son, and he said some things about you that I thought you might want to respond to. If you'd prefer, I could go straight to the police with what I learned."

She pursed her lips as she considered my words. She clearly wanted to push me out of the way and slam the door in my face, but she couldn't let me leave without learning what Justin had told me. Finally, she held the door open wider and gestured for me to come inside.

Her home was as big inside as it had looked outside. The front door led to a foyer with marble flooring and a pair of winding staircases on either side that led up to the second floor. A glittering chandelier hung from the ceiling, and artwork adorned all the walls. Even with my limited art history knowledge, the paintings looked expensive.

Dr. Li spun around on her heel and walked across the foyer, her bare feet silent on the marble. I hurried after her, cringing as my boots clopped across the floor.

She led me through to a gorgeous kitchen, like something out of a magazine: gleaming appliances, a double fridge, marble countertops, and a large bay window leading to the backyard. A marble-topped island stood in the middle of the kitchen, and she'd been making tea when I'd interrupted her.

"Tea?" she asked, gesturing to the display on the counter.

I nodded, and she poured out a cup for me from a porcelain teapot. She slid the teacup to me and gestured to another tray with milk and sugar in matching porcelain containers.

"Your home is beautiful, Dr. Li," I said, taking a look around the kitchen.

"Call me Deborah. So, what does that little weasel have to say about me?" she asked, settling onto a stool next to the island.

"Do you know him well?" I added milk and sugar to my tea and stirred the cup, the sound of the silver spoon against the porcelain echoing through the large room.

Deborah smiled and flicked a strand of hair out of her face. "This is a small town. You get to know everyone pretty well after some time. Justin and I weren't friends, of course, but obviously I knew his mother, so I got to know him too. Well enough to know that his pot addiction makes him an unreliable witness."

"You think he has an addiction? Can you even be addicted to weed?"

She rolled her eyes and smirked. "The research is still out, but if you're incapable of holding a job and spend all day on your couch because of the stuff, that sounds like an addiction to me."

"What about Gayle? How well did you know her?"

"As well as any doctor knows their nurse. Which is to say, not very well at all. She'd run tests for me and take the temperature of my patients before I saw them, but we didn't sit around the lobby gabbing about our shopping trips, if that's what you're asking."

Just then, a man entered the kitchen. "Has someone been shopping again?" he asked, walking over to Deborah and pulling her into a side hug. He gave her forehead a kiss, then turned to me, his smile wide. "This little lady sure does love her department stores."

"Geoff, stop," Deborah said, pushing him away, her smile wide.

Geoff had curly brown hair and dimples on each cheek. His skin was tan, though I had a feeling that was due to heritage rather than time spent in the sun. Dried paint marred his smooth hands, like he'd just come from painting a bedroom upstairs. A gold band flashed from his ring finger, and I spotted the matching diamond on Deborah's hand.

"Geoff Baker." He held out his hand. "I didn't realize we had guests."

"I just popped by to talk to Deborah," I said, returning the shake. "I didn't mean to interrupt your morning."

"Not at all," he said, sliding over to one of the stools by the island. "What are we talking about?"

"Actually, honey, Simone here is a patient, looking for some medical advice. Do you mind giving us a few minutes?" Deborah dropped her voice as she spoke to her husband, as if I couldn't hear them from across the table. Geoff flicked his eyes over to me, then back to Deborah, a smile growing across his face.

"Ah, work stuff, of course." He stood and pressed his hands together as he turned back to me. "Simone, it was great to meet you. Maybe I'll see you around town sometime. I have a painting to get back to."

Deborah and I watched him leave the kitchen. The only

sound that could be heard was the ticking of the grandfather clock in the foyer.

"He paints?"

Deborah nodded. "Most of the paintings in this house are his. Geoffrey Baker, ever heard of him?"

My eyes widened, even as I tried to play it cool. Of course I'd heard of Geoffrey Baker. He was only the hottest artist to come out of Seattle in the last twenty years.

"I didn't realize he lived in Pine Brook," I said, trying to smooth my features out to hide my surprise.

"He got his start in Seattle. It's where we met when I was doing my residency at Seattle General. When Liam first told me about the clinic he wanted to open in our hometown, I practically had to drag Geoff down here. But he's happier here, I can tell."

Did other people in town know that a famous painter was living in their midst? I hadn't heard anything about him since I'd moved to Pine Brook, so maybe everyone just knew him as Geoff Baker.

"He can get...protective of me," Deborah went on. "That's why I made up that story just now. Obviously, I didn't kill Gayle, but he was already anxious after the police visited. I didn't want to stress him out anymore. He's working on a commission for a dealer in Toronto, and he needs to focus right now."

"Do the police consider you a person of interest in Gayle's death?"

"What reason would I have to kill her? I wasn't friends with the woman, but she was good at her job. The kids always loved her, and she was usually able to create pretty strong bonds with our patients. She got them to trust her. She was very opinionated and liked things a certain way, and she wasn't afraid to stand up to Liam and me when she wanted things to go her way. Still, she was good at what she did. Now we have to find a new nurse. That's why I'm home now, instead of at the clinic. I've spent the morning reaching out to old colleagues to see if anyone knows of a nurse on the market." She gestured across the island to a laptop sitting open.

"The clinic is pretty packed right now. I'm surprised you'd stay home when it's so short-staffed."

She waved a hand flippantly. "Liam can handle it. Like I said, I'm looking for a new nurse. Besides, with Geoff antsy from the police visit, I didn't think it wise to leave him alone. He's very... sensitive."

She might've been telling me the truth, but it was also very possible that she was home because she couldn't face the clinic after murdering Gayle and was using her husband and the search for a new nurse as excuses. I didn't feel like fighting with her about that, though, so I moved on.

"Like I said before, I talked with Justin, and he said I should talk to you. He said you hated his mother. Is that true?"

Deborah's smile was genuine as she let out a laugh. "I mean, yeah. That's basically true. *Hate* is a strong word, but it wasn't a secret I thought Gayle was mean. But Liam wanted to keep her around, so I never made a fuss about it. Besides, Justin is trouble. He and his mom were always fighting. He's headed straight for jail or a grave. It's only a matter of time before he ends up in one or the other."

That matched with my interpretation of Justin. He did seem upset about his mother's death, but his tendencies leaned more towards the illegal.

"I'm surprised Gayle put up with him. I didn't know her well, but she didn't seem like the kind of person who would allow weed in her house," I said.

"Did you see that snake of his?" she asked. I nodded, holding in a shiver as I remembered its beady eyes.

"There were a lot of things in that house that I'm surprised Gayle allowed," Deborah went on.

"How do you know all this about their home life? I thought you weren't close with them."

She shrugged. "It's a small town, and we've worked together for years. You pick up on these things over time. Gayle always had a soft spot for her son. You can't blame her, of course, he was family, but you had to wonder whether she was holding him back by not forcing him to grow up."

Was it possible Gayle had tried to hold Justin accountable, and he'd responded with murder? Did he have the wherewithal to pull off something like this—stealing Estelle's pills, then sneaking them into his mother's system?

Just then, two wet snouts were shoved into my lap. I gave a jump at the intrusion, almost knocking over my teacup. Two giant black dogs had trotted in from the next room and were currently aggressively sniffing my crotch.

"Sorry about that." Deborah leaned over. "Thelma, Louise. Enough of that," she snapped. The two dogs pulled away from my lap and went to Deborah, sitting in front of her and staring up eagerly. She reached across the island to a small silver pot that I'd figured held more sugar, and pulled out treats for the dogs.

"They get excited about guests," she said.

The two animals, Bernese Mountain dogs, performed a cycle of tricks for her, sitting, moving into a down position, then rolling over on the floor. She tossed the treats at the dogs, and I discreetly wiped away dog slobber from my lap. What was it with this case and animals? Would I run into Big Bird at some point, too?

"So you're really trying to get to the truth of what happened?" Deborah asked, and I focused back on her. The dogs had now settled onto the ground in front of her, their heads flopped onto their paws as they watched me. "I saw something last week."

I waited for her to go on, then leaned forward when she didn't say anything more. "And?"

She scrunched up her nose and glanced down, her face pained. "I'm not sure if it's anything. But I don't want you thinking I had something to do with Gayle's death, so it's probably best if I tell you. Do you know Stella from Cuppa Joe's?"

The redheaded barista popped into my head, and I nodded.

Deborah glanced over her shoulder, as if checking to make sure Geoff hadn't come back into the kitchen. "Last week, I heard them arguing."

"It seems like they argue all the time. I don't really think that's news."

"No, this was different. It was like Gayle knew something about Stella that she didn't want to get out. And I saw them behind the coffee shop. You know how there's an alleyway that runs between all the buildings and lets out on Fourth Street? I was walking down Fourth and saw them back there. Gayle was all in Stella's face, wagging her finger at the poor woman, and then Stella started arguing back. That was surprising; normally, Stella keeps her cool with Gayle. I'll admit, I wanted to hear what they were saying, so I slowed down. I heard Stella say she was going to kill Gayle if she didn't stop bothering her."

My eyebrows shot up. "She said that? She said she was going to kill Gayle?"

"Well, I don't remember if she used the word 'kill,'

exactly. But it was something like '*I'll make you pay,*' or '*You'll regret this!*' Whatever it was, it was a threat. Stella is who you should be talking to right now." Deborah leaned back in her seat, looking mighty pleased with herself.

Stella probably thought they were alone in the alley. She may have threatened Gayle, and then, when Gayle didn't do what she wanted her to do, killed her a few days later. Could she have gotten a hold of Estelle's pills? When would she have had a chance to sneak them into Gayle's system? I wish I knew when exactly Gayle had ingested the pills!

"Did you tell the police about this?"

Deborah nodded. "Not sure if they'll do anything with the information, but I figured they should know."

"Well, thanks for your time." I stood, eager to find Stella and see what she had to say. She'd acted strange at the coffee shop that morning when the other barista had brought up Gayle's murder. Maybe she was more involved in all of this than I realized.

"Of course. I hope you find her killer. Regardless of how rude she could be, Gayle didn't deserve to die."

Deborah led me out of her home, and I took on a new appreciation for all the paintings on the wall as we walked. There was an artistic genius living in Pine Brook! Why weren't people in town talking about this more?

"Oh, actually, one more question," I said as she opened the front door. "I heard you and Liam used to date before you opened the clinic. Is that true?" While not totally relevant to Gayle's death, it was background information about the two doctors that might prove useful.

To my surprise, Deborah's cheeks turned pink, and she glanced away from me. Her hands started fidgeting.

"Oh, that. Yes. But it was years ago. Not interesting at all."

She held open the door and looked at me expectantly, so I left her home.

Outside, the rain clouds were still off in the distance, but the wind had picked up. I wrapped my jacket tighter around myself and dashed to my car. Deborah watched me from the front door as I got inside and pulled away from the curb, but she didn't shut the front door until I had turned the corner.

Why had she acted so strange when I brought up her relationship with Liam? Given how attractive and charming he was, you'd think she wouldn't have been embarrassed about that fact, even if she was married. Was there more going on than I realized? Had their relationship not really ended in high school?

Both doctors had indicated that they didn't mind working with Gayle, even if she was sometimes difficult. Was it possible they were both pretending that she wasn't that bad because Gayle knew something about them that they didn't want getting out? Did they have some secret going on at the clinic that she held over them to keep her job?

On the other hand, this lead on Stella was interesting. An argument days before someone was murdered wasn't necessarily an indication of guilt, but it opened up the pool of suspects. Of course, with Gayle, there was probably a long line of suspects I didn't even know about. Who else had she pissed off?

16

I parked my car on the side of the road a few blocks from the doctor's home, wanting to take a moment to pause and think about all that I'd learned so far. Deborah had pointed the finger at Stella, but that didn't mean I needed to run right off and ask the barista a million questions. Why would she even talk to me?

Besides, I couldn't shake the feeling of suspicion I still had about Deborah and Liam. They'd spent the most time with Gayle, so they'd had the most access to her, and they would've had easy access to Estelle's pills. If I could pin down the time that Estelle's pills had been taken, I might've been able to narrow the field of suspects, but Estelle hadn't remembered exactly when she'd lost them, as she didn't need to take them every day.

What about Gayle's time of death? When had the pills been introduced into her system? If I could figure that out from the police, I might have a better shot at eliminating some of these suspects. There was one person I could talk to who might've been able to help me figure out who was telling the truth and who was lying, and who might know when Gayle had been exposed to the soy supplements.

The Pine Brook Police Department was on the outskirts of town. I knew I was needed back at the inn, especially with Tracy still gone, but fortunately the police station was on the way. The three-story building housed a bullpen for the police officers, various offices for the top brass, a medical office for the medical examiner when she needed to see bodies in Pine Brook, and a small jail. I pulled up in front of the building and rang Detective Patel from my car.

Detective Monica Patel had been new to the Pine Brook force when I'd gotten to town and new to detective work in general. However, she'd worked hard to prove herself since arriving in Pine Brook. Solving four murders last year had given her some serious credit with the other officers and detectives. The police chief, Tate, still wasn't convinced of her competence, but last I heard, he was coming around.

"Hey, it's Simone," I said once she picked up my call. "I'm outside the station. Any chance you're around for a chat?"

Fifteen minutes later, Patel strode out of the police station, gripping a large black umbrella to protect herself from the rain. She spotted my car and dashed across the street. Her dark brown hair was tied back into a thick braid like it always was, and her brown skin was free of makeup, as usual, too.

"I can't talk about the Hart case," she said once she was inside the car.

"Well, hello to you, too," I said. "Feel free to turn up your heat if you're cold."

"Simone, I'm serious. I'm assuming that's why you're here, so I want to get ahead of anything and tell you I can't talk about it."

"I'm just here to see a friend. What's so wrong about that?"

She smiled at my use of the word *friend*, though she tried to hide it. "Nothing, except I know that's not true. You've been snooping around, trying to clear your friend, Estelle, and you're hoping to pump me for information."

I grimaced. "Who told you?"

"No one." She let out a chuckle. "I just know you well enough to know you aren't going to sit by while we question someone close to you. I remember how the last few murder cases in Pine Brook have gone."

She was right; I did have a tendency to get involved when I felt that the police were looking in the wrong direction.

"You can't fault me for wanting to help my friends, can you?"

"No." She shot her gaze at me. "But I can if it creates any trouble for my investigation. I got a call from Justin Hart, wanting to know what we were doing with his mother's case since someone had come around asking questions. He was vague when he described you, but when he said, 'the pretty Black woman,' I had a good idea of who he was talking about. You shouldn't bother a grieving child."

"I wasn't bothering him. I just wanted to see how he was doing. I'm surprised he called the police; he seemed more focused on Animal Planet than anything else."

"Whatever you said to him seemed to snap him awake. He'd been pretty closed-off before, not wanting to talk about his mother and even struggling to believe that she'd been murdered. After your little chat, he was much more forthcoming. I've got plans to see him later this week and go through his statement again."

"That's good; maybe he'll have something to share."

"Okay, enough dancing around the subject. What have you learned?"

I told her about Maria running off, Justin's snake and his belief that Deborah was involved, Deborah's denial of everything, and then the way she pointed the finger at Stella.

"Did you know Deborah's husband is that painter? Geoffrey Baker?"

Patel nodded. "I went to a few of his shows when I was living in Seattle. He's pretty talented. I didn't realize he was married to Deborah until we ran a background check on her, and he popped up on her social media. They don't talk about it much. I'm not sure why."

"Yeah, Deborah didn't want to discuss the case in front of him. She told him some lie about why I was there and made him leave the room."

"That's not so suspicious. If she's innocent, she may not want to expose him to all this questioning."

Patel had a point. Was Deborah simply trying to protect her husband? Or did she know that he might be able to prove that she was, in fact, guilty? Had he seen something that would indicate her guilt?

"Also, I was at Cuppa Joe's this morning, talking to one of the baristas about Gayle's death. He mentioned that he heard the police thought it was murder. Stella overheard and bolted out of the room. It's not much to go on, but coupled with the fight Deborah had seen, it might be worth following up on."

"Why can't you just go around this town and not talk to people about murder? Would that be so hard to do?"

I shrugged. "I'm just trying to help. It's not my fault if people keep telling me things, is it?"

Patel rolled her eyes but made a note. "I'll have someone follow up with Stella and see if she knows anything."

"I do wonder if Gayle had something on the doctors, and that's why they wouldn't fire her. Both of them have admitted that she was good at her job in certain ways, but I just can't imagine working with someone so unpleasant if I had the power to fire them."

"What do you think she had on them?"

I stared off to the side for a moment, thinking. "I'm not sure. It's not a very strong line of thinking, I know, but it just seems strange to me that they'd keep her employed."

"This is a small town. There aren't a lot of jobs. Maybe they felt bad and didn't want to take her job away from her."

"Maybe...Okay, that's all I know," I said. "Is there anything you can tell me?"

"Honestly, I shouldn't even be in here talking to you right now. You're not a cop, and this is an active investigation. Tate would have my head if he knew how much I've shared with you in the past."

My energy deflated. I'd been so hopeful that Patel would be able to tell me something that might get me closer to the killer, but if she wasn't willing to talk to me at all, then I was out of luck. She was a cop, and I was a civilian; she didn't have to tell me anything, but it was still discouraging.

I shifted in my seat. My back was still hurting a bit. I'd left the painkillers at home, as I didn't want to get in the habit of taking them, but I did feel like I could use one right now.

She sighed, drawing my attention back to her. "But why do I even try? You're just going to keep asking around, sticking your nose where it doesn't belong. Plus, you have been a help in the past. I may as well give you something to work with."

I held back my gleeful smile, not wanting to give her any reason to regret opening up to me.

"The medical examiner had some trouble pinning down the time of death. The pills that were introduced into Gayle's system, they didn't kill her right away. It can sometimes take up to two hours for an allergic reaction to hit. The M.E. said the pills were probably mixed with something Gayle had eaten that morning."

"I saw her at Cuppa Joe's that morning. She was getting a cup of coffee. Could they have been mixed into the coffee?"

Patel nodded. "There would probably be a slight bitter taste from the pills, but coffee could mask the taste. Also, since Gayle's allergy was so severe, the killer didn't need to put too much into her system, so she may not have tasted them if they were in her coffee."

"Was there anything else in her stomach? Could the killer have slipped the pills into something else she ate?"

"Dr. Haynes found a banana in her stomach, but we can't figure out how someone would sneak pills into a banana, so yes, we're assuming the pills were added to her coffee."

"When I saw her that morning, she said she always got coffee at Cuppa Joe's before coming into work. Does it mean someone put them into her coffee then?" Had Stella, or someone else, snuck something into her coffee cup that morning?

Patel shook her head. "Not exactly. Yes, Gayle always had a cup at Cuppa Joe's in the morning before work, but then she usually had her first cup at home, before she left for the day, and then again when she got into the office. The pills could've been added to any one of those coffees, which means any of the people most likely to kill her could've spiked her coffee at any point in the day. Justin could've given it to her in the morning when they were home, this Stella woman, or anyone else, could've done it at Cuppa

Joe's, if they swiped her cup before she grabbed it, or anyone at the clinic could've done it."

All my suspects went flying out the window. Any one of them could've killed Gayle. How were we going to pin down the killer?

"What are you going to do now?" I asked.

"Keep looking." Patel grimaced. "It's the only thing I can do right now. Her killer made a mistake somewhere. They always do. Now it's just a matter of finding that mistake and uncovering the truth."

"Good luck with that. I can't imagine having to do this all the time."

"Well, you don't get into this kind of work without knowing what to expect. I've always loved puzzles. When I was a kid, my brother and I would see who could put together a thousand-piece puzzle first. I usually won. My brother is now a teacher."

"You have a brother? Where does he live?"

"Seattle. I don't talk about him much. Now, obviously, finding all the pieces to create an image of the Grand Canyon isn't the same as finding a killer, but I believe I was meant to do this. And I'm not going to let this guy get away with murder."

"You think it was a guy?"

She shrugged. "It's just a saying. As we've seen, it could just as easily have been a woman. There's a lot more death in this town than I expected when I first arrived."

She didn't have to tell me twice. You'd think, in a town of this size, people would flee with all this death. But no one seemed to mind it all that much, or at least weren't willing to put in the effort to uproot their lives because of a few deaths.

"Speaking of more death, do you have any more information about the other body that was found by the creek? Do you think it's related to Gayle's death?"

Patel's face shut down, like she'd pulled a mask over her head to hide her emotions, and she leaned back in her seat. "I can't really talk about it. Like I said before, it looks like a drug overdose. Tragic, but not murder, and not related to Gayle's death. The woman had a drug addiction."

The newspaper had told me as much, but I'd been hoping Patel might have more intel to share. Still, the existence of two deaths didn't mean they were related. I could be barking up the wrong tree by asking about the overdose death, when Gayle's death had nothing to do with the other victim.

"I should probably get going," Patel said. "Whatever you're going to do, be careful. Don't forget that there's a killer out there. I may not be able to stop you from poking your nose into things that don't concern you, but I can at least warn you."

"Thanks."

"Is there anything else?" Patel had her hand on the door handle, looking ready to jump out of the car.

I shook my head. "No. Thanks for sharing all that about when the soy supplements were put into her system. I'll be sure to keep that in mind."

Patel left my car, slamming the door shut behind her. I put both hands on the steering wheel and stared out the window, watching her return to the police station.

My phone buzzed in my pocket, startling me. I slipped it out of my pocket and glanced at the screen.

Hey Simone, it's Justin. Could we talk? I think I have something to share about my mother's death. Meet me at my place tomorrow morning?

Why was Justin texting me? Where had he gotten my number? And what information did he have to share?

Patel was already inside the police station, and the street was quiet, the only sound in the car the patter of rain against the roof. Should I tell her about this text? Even though Justin had been more forthcoming with the police, he'd also been spooked about them when I'd talked to him. His weed, while possibly legal, was still excessive. I didn't want to scare him by showing up at his house with a police officer.

I'd go talk to him myself, and, if he had anything useful to share, I'd bring it straight back to Patel.

I typed out a quick message, agreeing to meet in the morning, then pulled away from the curb. All that was left for me to do was to go back to the inn and wait to see him in the morning.

If only I'd gone straight to his house as soon as he'd texted, things might've turned out differently for us all.

17

The next morning, I wasted no time in heading straight to Justin's house early. I didn't even know if he was likely to be awake this early, the sun barely poking its head over the horizon, but I didn't want to give him a chance to decide not to speak with me.

Before I left my apartment, my phone rang—a call from Nick. I hesitated, my finger hovering over the *Answer* button. We'd left things so awkwardly the last time we'd talked; didn't he deserve the opportunity to explain himself?

Then I thought about his girlfriend currently staying at my inn, and I ignored the call. Even if they were split up, I wasn't interested in getting involved with someone who wasn't honest about their past. I'd told Nick about my previous relationships, and he knew how betrayed I'd been by the cheating. It was hard to believe he could hear all that and not think it necessary to tell me about this complicated ex.

Rain clouds rolled in as I drove from my apartment, and they began dumping rain onto the town as I headed in Justin's direction. My windshield wipers worked double-time, slashing away the rain but getting dumped on again in the next second. I leaned in closer to the windshield, struggling to see out the window.

Traffic was heavy as I drove. Rain slowed all the cars down, and I passed a fender-bender on the side of the road near downtown. This rain was going to get someone killed if we weren't careful.

Finally, I pulled up in front of Justin's house. The traffic had made this trip three times longer than it should have been. Had I missed him? His car was still parked on the street in front of the house, though all the blinds over the windows were closed, and the house was quiet.

I didn't know if this was too early for him, so I decided to give him a call first to see if he was awake. I pulled out my phone and dialed the number he'd texted me from. No answer.

"Hey, Justin, it's Simone. I'm at your place. Did you still want to talk? Call me back as soon as you get this." I hung up the voicemail and set my phone on the seat next to me.

Peering out the car's window, I strained to see any movement inside his home. The blinds were pulled down, like they had been when I'd visited before, and the entire house sat like it was empty. No movement, no sounds. The whole street was silent. The rain had probably driven people inside. Was Justin still here?

"He wouldn't have gone anywhere in this rain without his car, right?" I muttered to myself. "He probably just stepped away from his phone and didn't see my call."

I looked back at my phone, willing him to call me back, but it was as silent as the house.

Sighing, I switched off the engine. There was only one way to know for sure where he was. Grabbing my phone and tossing my raincoat over my sweater, I dashed out of my car and up to his front door.

The plants in Gayle's garden were soaked. Muddy foot-prints led up to and away from the front door, and there was mud caked onto the small porch, though the rainstorm was beginning to wash them away. So, Justin was home. He probably sent me that message last night, then took a hit from his bong and passed out. Hopefully, he'd answer the front door.

I knocked, then shot backwards as the door swung open at my knock. I almost slipped off the edge of the porch at the surprise, and my arms pinwheeled out to my sides to keep my balance. Why was the door open? Had Justin left the house and forgotten to shut it properly?

Taking a step closer to the door, I poked my head through the gap and glanced around, but I couldn't see much of anything from this angle. I sighed, contem-plating my choices. It wasn't breaking in if the door was open, and he'd already invited me over, right? Besides, his Toyota was here. He probably forgot to shut the door completely and would be waiting for me inside.

"Justin?" I called out. "It's Simone. Are you here?"

I pushed the door open wider. No sign of Justin. I stamped my feet against the welcome mat to clear off any mud, then stepped inside his home.

The smell of weed still hung in the air, though it smelled different than it had the last time I was here. I sniffed the air. It smelled staler, like it'd been sitting in the air for several hours. Had he not smoked today?

The living room was empty, the TV on but muted. The closed blinds blocked out any light that might've come through, and I squinted as I walked through the house, trying to see anything. I also kept my gaze out for Priscilla the snake.

"Justin? Sorry for just walking in like this, but the door was open..." Still no answer. Had he left without his car?

I stepped into the back hallway, keeping my eyes peeled for any movement. No word from Justin, and I was beginning to think I'd entered his home without an invitation for no reason. Maybe he was passed out on his bed?

As I entered the back part of the house, a tangy smell hung in the air. I paused, sniffing. It smelled like... pennies?

Oh, no. I knew what that smell was. A tight ball of fear was blooming in my chest. I strode over to the first door in the hallway and pushed it open. Bathroom, empty.

The next door led to what I guessed had been Gayle's room. Made bedspread, floral pattern, floral curtains closed against the windows, several books stacked on her nightstand. It was like she'd left for the day knowing she'd never come back, but the room was always waiting for her.

I stumbled back out of the room, the scent of pennies now caught in my throat. One more door to go. This door was cracked open. Already, I could tell I was about to walk into something I'd regret. Taking a deep breath, I pushed open the door.

Full-size bed. Black sheets. Blackout curtains giving the room a dark shadow. Clothes scattered across the floor. Bong just barely spotted on the bedside table.

And on the bed: a body. Pale, sprawled across the sheets. Head turned to the side at an unnatural angle. The smell of blood hung in the air, and I quickly scanned the body, looking for a source.

The wrists: coated in something, though it was so dark in the room, I couldn't make out what it was. Eyes closed. Justin wasn't getting up again.

. . .

I STUMBLED out of the room, tripping over clothes and banging into a dresser as I went. I found my phone in my pocket and quickly dialed.

A short while later, I sat on the couch in the living room, staring at the scratched-up coffee table. Police officers filled the small room. Officer Scott and Detective Patel entered the house, quickly spotting me on the couch and hurrying over.

"Coming out!" said a voice from the hallway. We all swiveled around to watch.

Why were they removing the body so quickly? The police had only shown up a short while ago, and typically they spent more time at the crime scene studying the placement of the body before removing it. Plus, Patel would've wanted to see the body in the context of its death. I hated that I knew all that.

Justin. It was Justin's body. Referring to it as "it" wouldn't make the reality any different. I'd heard of cops and medical professionals aiming for objectivity when dealing with death, but I couldn't do that. It just made me hurt inside.

Why hadn't I gone inside the police station yesterday and told Patel about Justin's text? If I'd told her, she would've come with me to see him, and maybe we could've saved him. There wouldn't have been two deaths in this murder investigation.

"Clear the path." It was that voice again, from the hallway.

Two people wheeled something down the hallway and through the living room. Two EMTs on either side of what looked like a stretcher. I stood as realization washed over me.

They were wheeling out Justin on a stretcher. He was

hooked up to some medical apparatus, his torso coated in blood. But he was alive. My eyes filled with tears. *He was alive.*

"Simone, can we ask you a few questions?" Patel had approached with Officer Scott.

I turned to them, my mind racing. "He's alive?"

Patel hesitated, then nodded. "Yes. You didn't realize that when you called it in?"

I shook my head. "I...I just saw so much blood. It smelled...awful. But he...he's alive."

I wrapped my arms around my body and took a shuddering breath. I'd spent so much time around death since coming to Pine Brook, I'd just assumed I was seeing more of it. But this, this was different.

"Will you get her a bottle of water from my car?" Patel muttered to Scott, who scurried off to the front door. "Let's take a seat." Patel reached out and guided me back down to the couch. "Unless you'd like to speak back at the station? I know you saw something pretty horrific back there, and we can go somewhere else if you'd like."

I shook my head. "No, this is fine. Watch out for Priscilla." I tensed up, scanning the floor for the snake.

"Is that the snake? Don't worry, we caught her." Patel gestured over her shoulder to another officer who was cradling the snake like Britney Spears at the 2001 VMAs. I shuddered at the image.

"Ricardo has a thing for snakes," Patel went on. "He'll make sure she's taken care of until Justin can come back home. Now, tell me what you're doing here. Why did you come here this morning?" She pulled out her notepad and a pen.

"Justin, he...he sent me a text. He said he had something to tell me, and he asked to meet."

Patel narrowed her eyes. "And you didn't think to tell me about this?"

I shrunk back. "I didn't know why he wanted to talk. I wasn't sure if it had anything to do with his mother's death, or something else. Plus, I wasn't sure if he would talk to me if I showed up with a cop. He smokes a lot, and yes, it's legal in Washington, but I can't imagine everything he has here is perfectly legal."

Even with legalization, people still got their weed through drug dealers or other nefarious methods. I'd read about it in the paper. Legalization put in place rules and taxes, and long-time users didn't want to deal with that. So, they kept up their contacts and purchased what they could.

Most had started getting their weed through legal means, but Justin seemed like someone who wouldn't want to have to register with the state, given his hesitancy about talking to the police when I'd brought it up.

"Can I see the text?"

I nodded and slipped my phone out of my pocket, unlocking it and finding the message from Justin. I passed the phone to Patel, who let out a deep sigh as she read it. Officer Scott came into the room and passed me a water bottle, then went to stand a few feet away. I took a grateful sip.

"I really wish you'd told me about this yesterday." Patel passed me back my phone, then stood and stopped one of the officers walking past us. "Make sure there's extra security on Mr. Hart's room at the hospital, okay? I want someone with him the entire time he's at that hospital." The officer nodded and strode away. Patel sat back down, turning back to me. "Tell me what you saw when you got here."

I took a deep breath to steady myself, then walked her through what happened when I arrived. I told her about the door being partially open and the darkness inside the house. I also mentioned that I saw Justin's car parked on the street, but that the house was silent and smelled like stale weed. Then I told her about finding his room and seeing all the blood.

"I was certain he was dead."

Patel scratched some notes into her notepad. "If you hadn't come by when you did, he would've succumbed to his injuries. Simone, you saved him."

Tears filled my eyes and fell onto my cheeks. I hung my head at the sudden emotion, taking deep breaths to try to steady myself. I'd saved him. I'd saved somebody.

"What happened to him? I didn't get a good look, but it didn't seem good."

Patel lowered her voice. "It looks like he may have tried to kill himself. We're looking for a note now, but it appears that he tried to take his life."

Had Justin seemed suicidal when I first talked to him? He'd definitely been upset about his mother's death, but did that mean he'd tried to take his own life? What if I hadn't shown up when I did?

"I think we're done with questions for now." Patel's voice was gentle. She patted my arm, smiling softly. "You did a good thing here. Do you need a ride home?"

I shook my head. "I have my car. Don't worry, I can drive," I added in response to her unspoken question. "I just need a minute, but I can drive myself."

Patel nodded and stood. "We'll have you come to the station tomorrow to sign your statement. And please, no running off to any potential suspect's home without telling me first."

She left me on the couch to confer with the other officers, and I stared at my lap, trying to reconcile all my thoughts. The police were still looking for a note. If they find something, it might explain what had happened to Justin.

Did he try to kill himself because he was distraught over his mother's death? Was he actually responsible for his mother's death, and couldn't live with the guilt? Or did the killer just want us to think that? It couldn't have been a coincidence that he'd sent me that text, could it? I needed to speak with him as soon as possible and get answers about what had happened.

18

Pine Brook Memorial Hospital was a large, three-story building near downtown. Glass windows lined the second and third stories, reflecting the sun and raising the temperature in the area around the hospital. The morning after stumbling onto Justin's bloody body, I pulled into the visitor's parking lot and walked up the shrub-lined path to the front doors of the hospital, which swooshed open as I approached.

Before leaving Justin's home the day before, I'd chatted with one of the officers who'd been standing outside watching the ambulance leave.

"Are they taking him to Pine Brook Memorial?" I had asked, gesturing towards the ambulance. There was only one hospital in town, but I wanted to make sure I went to the right place. "I want to check on how he's doing. With his mother gone, I just want to make sure he knows he's not alone." I crossed my fingers behind my back like a seven-year-old. She didn't need to know that I was really going to see if he had any idea about who hurt him.

"That's right," she said, nodding towards the ambulance

that was now fading in the distance. "You probably can't visit him yet, but I'd call to check."

I'd tried calling the day before, after leaving Justin's house, but the stern man on the phone had told me that there would be no visitors until after Justin came out of surgery. I'd spent the night wracked with guilt, wondering if I could've stopped this by showing up to his house sooner. What did he know that led to this attack? What had he been planning to tell me?

Before leaving that morning, I'd dropped off Lola with Nadia at the inn. I had a feeling I was going to be out late today snooping, and I wanted to make sure someone kept an eye on Lola for me. With Tracy gone and Estelle and Miles fretting about a murder charge, Nadia was my best bet for keeping an eye on Lola. The guests loved her, so I didn't think anyone would mind.

"Just be careful, okay?" Nadia said, taking the leash and leading Lola back to the front desk.

"I promise!" I called after her.

As I'd left my apartment that morning on my way to see Justin, I'd spotted Nick in the lobby as I'd come down the stairs. I'd waited at the top for him to leave the lobby before continuing down. I knew I was being stubborn by avoiding him like this, but I didn't want to get hurt again by getting involved with someone who couldn't tell me the truth. Besides, I had a murderer to catch and no time to discuss my feelings.

The hospital smelled like antiseptic and bleach. The walls were an off-white and the overhead lighting was unflattering to anyone who walked below it. I'd called again that morning and been told that Justin had been moved to the ICU, so I followed the signs pointing along the walls.

The longer I thought about what had happened yesterday, the more convinced I was that Justin hadn't tried to kill himself. He'd been attacked by the person who'd killed his mother, and it was only through sheer luck that I'd gotten to him before his injuries turned fatal.

I'd started snooping around this case to help Estelle, but it was clear now that this killer needed to be brought to justice. Justin, while a slacker, hadn't done anything to hurt anyone else, and I now felt compelled to stop whoever had done this to him.

In the hospital, I passed mostly closed doors, though the few that were open looked in on small rooms with windows and whirring machines. TVs set to low volume chattered in the corners of some rooms, while others had low voices floating into the hallway. I ignored the tightness in my stomach—hospitals always gave me the heebie-jeebies—and pressed on.

"Excuse me," I said to a nurse seated at a workstation in the middle of the hallway. I'd found the area Justin was in, but I didn't know which room was his. "I'm looking for Justin Hart."

The nurse, her dark hair pulled back into a severe bun and her brown skin looking tired, pointed over my shoulder. I turned and spotted a police officer standing in front of one of the doors, his hands on his belt, staring straight ahead. I was startled as I realized Deborah was in front of the man, arguing with him. Well, arguing *to* him. The police officer barely noticed she was there. What was she doing here?

I strolled over to where they were standing, trying to look casual as I got closer to hear what Deborah was saying. She was clutching a bouquet of flowers, and she looked pissed.

"I don't know who gave you the right to turn people away, but that poor boy has lost his mother and doesn't have any other family. I need to see him." Her voice was raised, and she was leaning in close to the officer, but he wasn't budging. Since when did Deborah care so much about Justin? Was she here to finish him off?

"Ma'am, I'm sorry, but I cannot let you in," the officer said finally, his deep baritone jarring with his baby-faced looks.

"What's going on?" I asked, unable to keep myself away. Both heads swiveled in my direction, and Deborah's eyes widened as she saw me.

"Apologies for the confusion," a new voice said, and the three of us turned to see a doctor approaching. "I'm Dr. Lancaster, Justin's surgeon," he explained once he was at the door. He was Black, with a shaved head and a broad chest. "We were told by the police not to let anyone in. Besides, Justin is, unfortunately, in a coma right now, so he's not seeing anyone. Are you family?"

Deborah and I both shook our heads no. Based on the look on her face, she was just as surprised as I was to learn that Justin was in a coma. Had his attack really been that bad?

"Is he going to survive?" I asked.

"I'm a doctor," Deborah said, butting in ahead of me. "His mother worked for me and was recently killed. I'm here to check on him."

"Or here to finish him off," I spat out. I was tired of her holier-than-thou attitude, and I knew how she really felt about him. If she had been involved in his attack or in his mother's death, we couldn't let her anywhere near him.

Dr. Lancaster looked between the two of us, then up at the police officer in front of the door. "I think it's best if you both leave now," he said finally, gesturing us away from the door.

I sent one look back at Justin's door but agreed and moved away. Once Deborah and I were out of sight of the police officer and doctor, she turned on me.

"Why would you say that? I was going to get in there. Justin shouldn't be alone right now, even if he is in a coma." She stumbled over the last word as if the reality of it was too much to handle.

"I can't let you in if you're here to hurt him. How did you even know he was here?"

"I have a friend at the hospital who knew Gayle worked for me and called me when she found out that Justin was brought in after a suicide attempt. I came as soon as I could. What are you doing here?"

"I found him yesterday. I came to check on him."

We stared at each other for a few moments, seemingly trying to decide if the other was a threat. After a moment, Deborah relaxed and let the flowers droop by her side, so I let my defenses down, too. Who attacks someone and makes it look like a suicide, then shows up at their bedside the next day with flowers? Even if she was the killer, she wasn't getting in to see him today.

"That's not true, what you said about me," she said, taking a seat on one of the chairs lining the walls. "I'm not here to hurt Justin. I just want to make sure he's safe."

I took a seat next to her. "I thought you didn't like him? He sure didn't like you."

"Yeah, well, we can't all be well liked." She sighed and slouched down in her seat, all her energy gone. "Listen, you were right about me and Gayle. She did know something about me. But it's not what you think." She paused, then took a deep breath. "I'm thinking about leaving the clinic. Geoff wants to travel, and he's never liked Liam. I've been trying to work up the courage to tell Liam, and Gayle over-heard me on the phone with Geoff talking about it."

My eyes widened at her words. "So you were going to leave Liam? When were you going to tell him?"

She shrugged. "I'm not sure. Right before Geoff and I left town? That's a bit of an exaggeration, since our joint owner-ship would draw things out, but I wasn't eager to tell him before I had to. Liam and I have such a history together, I didn't think he'd take it well. But I never would've hurt Gayle over that information. She loved her secrets, but she wasn't ever going to do anything with it. She just liked having the information. She didn't care what anyone thought of her and was always willing to make her opinions known, especially when she tried to do what was best for the patients. I respected that."

Could I believe Deborah? I hadn't found any evidence that she was leaving the clinic, but I hadn't dug very deep into her personal life. That might've explained why she looked so uncomfortable when I brought up her former relationship with Liam; she was ashamed that she might be hurting him by leaving, especially given that they had such a long history together.

"Why did you say I was here trying to finish him off?" Deborah asked, breaking into my thoughts. "He tried to kill himself, and I'm just trying to make sure he's okay."

I hesitated, knowing that Patel wouldn't want me to share this information, but also needing to see if I could catch Deborah in a lie. Besides, if she wasn't the killer, which I was becoming less and less certain of, she might know something that could help with the case.

I leaned in and lowered my voice, not wanting the police officer standing guard in front of Justin's door to hear me. "I'm not so sure if this was suicide. I think Justin was attacked by the same person who killed his mother, and they tried to make it look self-inflicted."

Deborah's eyes widened, and she reared back from me as if I'd slapped her. She swore. "You honestly can't believe I'd do that to him? I'm a doctor, for goodness sake!"

"Doctors aren't infallible."

She scoffed. "When was he attacked? What time?"

"Um, I'm not sure," I said, thinking back to what the police had said yesterday. "He asked to meet me. He texted me the night before, on Saturday, and we agreed to meet the following morning, on Sunday, yesterday. So, I'd guess sometime in between those times."

"Well, that's easy then," Deborah said, sitting up in her seat and turning more fully to me. "Geoff and I spent the night at his art show in Seattle. I was there all night with him, and we stayed the night at a hotel. Hundreds of people probably saw me. I can get you some names if that would get you off my case."

It was hard to make up hundreds of witnesses. "I'm not the police, but you should tell Detective Patel about that. She's probably already at your house wanting to question you. I might've mentioned that you two had some bad history."

Deborah rolled her eyes. "Please come to me, if you have a problem with me, before telling the police. I'd rather not be accused of another murder."

"I'm sorry." I paused, my thoughts still on Justin's attack. "If you were out of town two nights ago, that means Liam might've been in town alone. Do you know if he has an alibi for Justin's attack?"

"Hey, I won't have you going around accusing me or my business partner of murder." Her eyes flashed, suddenly full of anger. I cringed, shifting away from her.

"Not that it's any of your business," she went on, "but Liam was at a conference in Seattle all night on Saturday, and he didn't leave until the morning. You have to check in with someone at those things, and they usually track where your car is. I'm sure hundreds of people saw him that night. Now, keep your nose out of things that don't concern you."

19

The rain had stopped by the time I left the hospital. The sky was still gray but the air was fresh, and I took a deep breath as I exited the building. The scent of antiseptic and decay had followed me out of the building, and I wanted to give myself some time to clear the cobwebs from my head.

After Deborah had left the hospital, I'd hung about for a little while longer, but no one was getting in to see Justin. Besides, he wasn't telling anyone about what had happened to him or who had done this to him. Was the truth buried somewhere inside him, yet he couldn't tell the world? It broke my heart to know that the person who had harmed him and his mother was still out there. I was even more determined to find the truth.

Outside the hospital, a paved pathway led around the side of the building and connected with a park just off the town square. Few children were at the park, given the rain and the fact it was a school day, and I found my thoughts wandering as I strolled down the pathway.

Benches lined the pathway, with bushes scattered along

the way. Few flowers were blooming at this time of year, but would undoubtedly lend a cheerful presence once fully sprouted. It might've made it easier for the loved ones of people in the hospital, giving them a place to go while worrying about the health of someone they cared for.

A figure was seated on one of the benches, their head buried in their hands. As I approached, their blond hair and large hands morphed into someone I recognized.

"Liam?" I called out once I was a couple of feet away.

Liam looked up, his eyes wide as he scanned the pathway for the source of his name. For a moment, our eyes locked on each other, and I could've sworn I saw fear in his face. Then he blinked, his features smoothed out, and his lips curved into a smile. He stood and met me down the path.

"Simone, you surprised me." His tone was jovial, his hands casually tucked into the pockets of his tan pants. "I didn't expect to run into anyone out here."

"Sorry for scaring you. Were you going into the hospital to see Justin?" Was he worried about the younger man? Did that explain the fear that had briefly come over his features?

"I stopped by already. I'm so shocked to think he'd try to kill himself. I wanted to check on him, but it looks like they aren't letting in visitors." He ran a shaky hand through his hair, then tried to play it off by quickly shoving his hand back into his pocket. "I was just taking a moment to think out here before heading back to the clinic. Deborah mentioned that you stopped by her place and talked to her. Are you still trying to figure out what happened to Gayle?"

I didn't want the killer to know what I was doing, but I didn't want to lie, either. Liam didn't need to know exactly what I was up to, just that I cared about his nurse and her son.

"I wouldn't exactly say I'm trying to figure out what happened. Honestly, I can't really explain it, but I feel compelled to help since we were the ones to find Gayle's body. Have you thought of anything else that might be pertinent to their case? Any reason why someone would want to hurt Gayle?"

Liam looked off into the distance, thinking, then shook his head and turned back to me. "Not at all. I've been thinking about it ever since it happened, but it just doesn't make any sense. Gayle wasn't the nicest person in town, but she never meant anyone any ill-will. Justin, on the other hand... I'm surprised he wasn't the one killed, instead of his mother."

"Really? What makes you say that?"

"Well, he was always getting into trouble. When he was in school, Gayle was always having to leave the clinic early to pick him up because he'd been suspended or had a parent-teacher conference to go over his 'issues.'" He added air quotes to the word "issues." "She didn't share much with me about what exactly was going on with him, but we could always tell something was up. Honestly, I wouldn't be surprised if it turned out that Gayle's death was caused by something Justin had done."

I raised my eyebrows. This was a new theory. "What do you mean?"

"Well, think about it." Liam leaned forward, pressing his hands together. "Justin's the one always getting into trouble with the law and with other people. Maybe he pissed off his drug dealer or owed someone money, so they went after his mother. It wouldn't be the first time an innocent family member got caught up in someone else's violent drama."

It was an interesting theory, but it didn't really hold water. If the killer was after Justin in the first place, why kill

Gayle in such an elaborate manner? They'd have to know about Estelle's soy supplements and Gayle's allergy, and also know that the two women had a history together that would lead the police to suspect Estelle. It was too much of a coincidence for that to have happened on its own.

"That's an interesting theory, but I'm not so sure about it," I said. "It seems like quite a reaction for some owed money. But what do I know? People have killed for less."

"Of course." Liam nodded. "You're probably right. I'm sure it's much less complicated than that. I just hate to think that Gayle might've done something to bring this onto herself. It's easier to believe that Justin played some role in everything, as I know he was always more likely to get into trouble with others."

I remembered the alibi Deborah had given for Liam. He clearly believed that Justin's wounds were self-inflicted, but I wanted to see if I could verify what she had told me.

"This is random, but Deborah mentioned you were at a conference or something on Saturday night? It sounded pretty interesting. What was it about?"

"Ah, yes, it was a medical conference on neural pathways in the elderly." He didn't seem to notice my out-of-the-blue segue. "It's not my professional focus, but I find the topic fascinating, and these conferences are always a great networking opportunity."

"Oh, I actually thought I saw you in town on Saturday night, but maybe that wasn't you," I said, the lie falling out smoothly. "Were you at the conference all night?"

He nodded. "You must've seen someone else in town. I didn't come back to Pine Brook until the following morning. We all had a few too many drinks, and I didn't think it was wise to drive back in my condition, so I got a room for myself."

"You're right, it must've been someone else. My mistake."

"How are you feeling, by the way?" he asked.

"A lot better," I said. I didn't add that this murder investigation was doing a good job of keeping me distracted from my back pain. "Those pain meds really helped, and so did taking a couple of days off. I guess I should listen to my friends when they tell me to go to the doctor when I'm hurting. I probably could have dealt with this a lot sooner."

"Eh, everyone's the same as you, even doctors. No one wants to admit they need help or that they might be sick. It's easier to just continue on like everything is okay." He glanced down at his watch. "Listen, I should probably get going. I need to get back to the clinic. We're a bit under-staffed now that we're down a nurse and a receptionist."

"Oh, I saw that there was someone else working the front desk a couple days ago. What happened to Maria?"

"It's the strangest thing, actually. We haven't heard from her in a few days. She's normally so punctual, but she's not answering her phone."

"Really? The last I saw her was when she ran off after I talked to her the day after Gayle's body was found. I thought she had acted strangely, but I hope nothing's wrong."

Liam tapped his finger against his chin, looking off to the side for a moment. "You know, she never came back to work after that day. I thought she was sick or something, but you think there's something else going on with her? I can't imagine what might've happened to her. Is she a part of all this and trying to keep it a secret? It doesn't make much sense."

"I don't know. But if you haven't heard from her in days, it seems like the police should probably increase their efforts to try to find her. If she didn't kill Gayle, maybe she knows who did and is hiding out from them." Or worse, I thought, but didn't say—maybe the killer got to her, too.

"Well, I hope the police can find her," Liam said. "I'd hate to think something has happened to her. I'll ask Deborah if she's heard from her, too, and I'll let you know what she says."

"Thanks, I appreciate that. Hey, listen, one more thing, before you go. I heard about this other death in town recently. I'm wondering if you were her doctor. Rebecca Hanlon, I think her name was. I guess it looks like a drug overdose? Does this sound familiar? It happened a few days before Gayle's death."

"Oh, I did hear about this, I think it was on the news. I wasn't her doctor, as she didn't come to the clinic. Not everyone in town does. Several doctors at the hospital take patients. She probably went to one of them. I'm sure the police have figured out who her doctor is by now. You could ask them."

"The police aren't always that forthcoming with sharing information with me. Which is understandable, they probably shouldn't, but it still makes it hard. Besides, I think because it was an overdose and not a murder, they aren't looking into it as closely. I just wondered if you knew anything."

"Sorry, not really. I wish I could help more. It's scary to think there's a killer out there. You have to wonder if we're safe here, you know?"

"That's true, but I'm sure the killer went after Gayle for a very specific reason. There would be more deaths if there was more of a danger to everyone else. I'm just going to try to stay out of the police's way and let them handle everything."

That wasn't completely honest, but Liam didn't need to

know that. And if he did end up going to the police with any information, I didn't want him thinking that I was snooping around, and I didn't want him telling the police that. It was better if everyone thought I was staying out of this one.

"Well, I should get going," Liam said. "Need to get back to the clinic and all. You be safe out there, okay?" He smiled, then turned on his heel and walked away.

I'd hoped by this point to learn more information about this other dead body in town, but it seemed like no one knew anything about her. Patel wasn't going to share anything with me, and I wanted to keep Estelle out of the investigation, even though she had good connections in town and could probably find out more. However, there was someone else I could call.

Miriam picked up on the third ring. I'd called her cell phone, rather than the police station, as she might've been more likely to share information with me if she wasn't using her work phone.

"It's Simone Evans. I'm looking into Gayle's death to help Estelle, and I wanted to see if you had any information about this other dead body that was found in town...the drug overdose. I don't know much about her."

"One second." A few moments passed in silence, then Miriam came back on the line. "Sorry about that. I'm in a broom closet. I wanted to get away from the front desk so that no one hears me. Now, what is it you want to know?"

Any concern I had about making Miriam do something she didn't want to do was wiped away, since she was calling me from a broom closet. Clearly, this woman loved the drama of these murder investigations and wanted to do whatever she could to share information with me.

"I was wondering if you knew anything about Rebecca Hanlon, the woman found dead by the creek recently. I'm trying to decide if it has anything to do with Gayle's death, since they both occurred around the same time, but I can't find any information on her."

"Oh, yes, I remember that," Miriam said. "Such a shame. She was a young woman, so full of life."

My heartbeat sped up at the sound of Miriam's words. "Does that mean you have information about her? Do you have access to her case file?"

"I can probably find it. What I remember is that she'd suffered from a drug overdose. Everyone here seems to think it was a tragic accident, but you're right that it's fishy that it happened right before Gayle died. Do you think they're related?"

"I don't know, but I want to look into her more. Can you text me her picture?"

"Of course. Anything to help Estelle. I'll let you know if I learn anything else!" We said our goodbyes and hung up, and I thought about what I was going to do next.

I wasn't going to get any more information out of Justin while the police were still guarding his room and he was in a coma, and I needed to check on things at the inn. Tracy was still out of town, and I wanted to make sure I didn't leave the staff alone for too long. I could ponder Justin's attack while I did some work.

Nadia had things under control at the front desk when I showed up, and Lola greeted me with a lick and a silent request for treats. I smiled and passed her a cookie, then strolled around the inn looking for some work to do. There was some laundry to be folded, which I was happy to do, and one of the hallways needed to be vacuumed. As I worked, I thought about the case.

I couldn't imagine what kind of person would have the confidence to try to kill someone and make it look like a suicide. That, coupled with the convoluted way Gayle was killed, implied that this person was smart and would do what they could to keep suspicion off of themselves. I'd have to be careful as I continued digging. I couldn't let them know what I suspected.

"Hi, there!" Suddenly, Nick's girlfriend was standing in front of me, a broad smile across her face. I reared back as if she'd slapped me, then quickly straightened my features to not look so scared. She was a guest, and I didn't want to freak her out, even if her presence made my palms sweat.

"Hi, yes, can I help you?" I asked, looping the vacuum's cord around its base.

"What time does the bistro open for lunch?"

"Um, noon, but you can probably go in early and see if there's anything left over from breakfast. We don't keep very strict hours down there."

"Awesome, thanks! I can't wait to try some of the produce Nick supplies for you all." She gave a tiny wave goodbye, then turned around and pranced down the hallway.

I sighed and lugged the vacuum back to the supply closet on this floor. Having to play nice with this woman while she stayed at the inn was getting on my nerves. Why wasn't Nick dealing with her? Did he even know she was here? This was why I didn't want to get involved with Nick; all these complications were more than I wanted to deal with.

My phone buzzed with a call, and I pulled it out of my pocket. Estelle's smiling face peered up from the screen.

"Hey, Estelle," I said, answering the call and shutting the door to the supply closet.

"Stella's the killer!"

"What? How do you know?"

"She's fleeing town! She must be guilty!"

It wasn't Estelle's best evidence she'd ever found. "How do you know she's fleeing? Maybe she has an appointment in another town."

"I was at Cuppa Joe's this morning, and one of the baristas mentioned that she hadn't shown up for work today. I didn't think much of it at first, but then someone else said that they saw her packing up her car today, like she was going on a trip or something. She must be trying to escape town, so I called you as soon as I could!"

"I dunno," I said slowly. "She could be packing her car for any number of reasons."

"I think I should go talk to her. Put the screws to her and see if she'll crack."

I rolled my eyes. Estelle had been watching too many noir detective films from the 1940s recently. "We should leave this to the police. You should be calling Patel right now, not me. I don't want anyone else getting hurt."

"Stella's not going to talk to the police! We're the only chance of finding the truth!"

Estelle's passion for being a detective was sometimes too much to handle. She might be right that Stella would be less likely to talk to the police if she were guilty. But I couldn't have Estelle doing something that might get her in trouble with the police.

"I'll go talk to her," I said, eager to get out of the inn with Nick's girlfriend running around. "You're still a suspect, and we don't want the police thinking you're trying to mess with their investigation. Do you know where Stella lives?"

"Yes! I'll text you her address."

We said our goodbyes and hung up, and I went in search of a raincoat. It wasn't much to go on, but was Stella fleeing town after attacking Justin? She wasn't very big, but Justin was a small guy—it wouldn't take much to overpower him.

Or was she fleeing town because she knew the identity of the real killer? I couldn't let her leave without finding out what she knew.

20

S tella lived not far from Estelle, near the downtown area. Her commute to Cuppa Joe's was probably pretty great. She lived in a small bungalow with a large oak tree in a postage-stamp-sized front yard. I rang the doorbell and looked around, spotting a car parked in the driveway. Looked like she hadn't left town yet.

No answer to the door. I leaned in to see if I could hear anything, but it was hard to tell through the thick door. I knocked again. A chill ran through me as I realized how similar this was to me finding Justin the day before. What would I find behind Stella's front door?

Was she even home? Had she left town already? Her car was here, but that didn't necessarily mean anything. Maybe she was at the back of the house and couldn't hear me. I decided to look for a backdoor.

Just as I was about to step off the porch and go around the side, the door swung open, revealing a dark interior and someone standing on the other side.

"What are you doing here?" Stella's voice was tight, like she was straining to get the words out.

I held my hands up in what I hoped was a placating gesture. "I just want to talk. Can I come in?"

Stella hesitated, glancing over her shoulder.

"Please, this'll only take a minute," I said. Her gaze was steady, though she looked like she was about to cry. Finally, she sighed and stepped to the side, letting me in.

The front door opened onto a small hallway. The hallway light was off, which explained why it was hard to see her in the doorway. Stella flicked on the switch and led me down the hallway.

The hallway opened up onto the living room, which was surprisingly bright and airy. A TV was pushed into one corner, with a couch and two armchairs squished around it. A dining room table was also shoved into the room. It was covered in papers, power cords, and empty glasses. I spotted a kitchen further down the house and figured there were bedrooms past the kitchen.

Standing in the middle of the living room, I turned to Stella, keeping my arms crossed as I studied her. She was chewing on one of her nails, her eyes were darting around the room and her arms were wrapped around herself. I followed her gaze and spotted a suitcase sitting open on the couch, half-full of clothes and other items.

"Going somewhere?" I nodded to the suitcase.

She sneered at me. "What's it to you? I can pack in my own house. What are you even doing here, anyway? You can't just barge into people's houses like this. I could call the police on you just for standing in here."

"You let me in the door," I said, taking a step closer to her. "But I don't think you're going to call the police. In fact, I think you don't want the police here at all. Don't want them snooping around, asking questions."

"What are you talking about?" she said, but her voice

had lost its bravado, and she wouldn't meet my eyes. I had her.

"There are rumors around town about what you did. I can understand how hurtful those rumors can be. People are talking about a fight you had with Gayle, and now her son's been attacked, too. I'm sure you didn't mean to hurt either of them, but the truth has to come out now. Did Justin know what you did to Gayle? Is that why you attacked him?"

"What are you talking about?" Her face had lost its fear, and she was now looking confused. I hesitated, unsure, then pressed ahead.

"Did you slip Gayle a pill because she wouldn't stop hassling your coffee shop? Your boss wouldn't help, so you had to take matters into your own hands. Estelle was always around; you could've easily swiped her pills."

Stella's jaw dropped open. "You think I killed Gayle? Is that why you're here?"

"Why else would you be leaving so suddenly?" I gestured to the suitcase, but I was losing my confidence. Her reaction was not what I had anticipated when I imagined confronting a killer. Her face was more incredulous than I would've expected.

Stella let out a bark of laughter, then slapped her hand over her mouth, as if to keep more hysterics from escaping. She sank down onto the couch and put her face into her hands. I glanced around, unsure of what to do. Was she about to cry?

"I didn't kill anyone," she said after a moment, looking up at me. Her eyes filled with tears, but she kept them from spilling over her face. "I suppose I can understand how you might think that. I did have a bad relationship with Gayle, but I wouldn't have hurt Justin. We went to high school together. He was an idiot, but he could be nice once you got to know him. He used to come into Cuppa Joe's, and we'd talk about snakes."

I shuddered as I remembered the snake in Justin's house. Did Stella have a snake, too? What a weird topic to talk about together.

"You're right about the police," Stella went on. She took a deep breath. "I am packing up because I need to get out of town. I've been stealing from Cuppa Joe's, and I'm afraid they're going to catch me."

Her words hung in the air between us, full of guilt and yet also the most honest thing she'd said all day.

"I can't keep lying anymore. I have to tell someone what's going on. My boyfriend, Jacob, he's making me do it. When I started working at Cuppa Joe's, I began working rotating shifts. Sometimes I open in the morning, other days I close at night. On the days that I closed, Jacob would come by at the end of the day and hang around, and he noticed how easy it would be to slip a few bucks from the register. So, we started doing it. Taking small amounts every couple of nights whenever I had a closing shift, no big deal. But then he wanted me to start taking more and more. I told him the boss would notice, and with the police sniffing around because of Gayle's death, it wasn't safe anymore. But he wouldn't listen. I'm packing up because Jacob is out of town at a gaming convention, and this is the only time I'll be able to get away from him."

She looked up at me, tears falling down her face, but her eyes were steely. I slowly walked over to the couch and took a seat next to her, reaching out my hand to grab hers, but she shrunk away from me. I let my hand fall into my lap.

"I understand the need to get away while Jacob is out of town, but you have to understand how guilty it makes you look if you leave," I said. "If the police learn you've skipped town during a murder investigation—especially after hearing about the big fight you and Gayle had before she died—they're going to think you were involved. But if you're not the real killer, then they'll be wasting their energy trying to find you, and the true killer will walk free. Plus, how are you going to stay gone with the police hunting you?"

Stella hesitated at my words, then shook her head and stood up. "I don't care what you say. I can't stay here. If Jacob comes back, he'll know what I was planning, and he'll...I don't know what he'll do. I can't be here."

I stood, following her around the room. "You need to go to the police. They can protect you. If you tell them what he's been making you do, they'll want to go after him, and you'll probably get off more easily. You're well-liked in this town; people won't want to see you in jail."

"Oh, yeah, because the police are so known for their protection skills. I watch the news; seems like these days, you go to the police and you get hurt." Her face was hard.

"Detective Patel is different. She can help you get the help you need. Running like this, you'll just look guilty, and you'll be looking over your shoulder for the rest of your life."

Stella broke down, tears streaming down her face, her thin shoulders shaking from her cries. I reached out and pulled her into a hug, patting her back and making soothing sounds.

"I never wanted this," she said after a moment, pulling away and wiping at her nose with her arm. I glanced around and spotted a box of tissues on the side table, so I grabbed a few and passed them to her.

"Thanks," she said, blowing her nose. "I never wanted this," she repeated. "It was all Jacob's idea. We've been together since high school, and he made it seem like this would be a victimless crime. My boss is a jerk and deserves what's coming to him, but every time I would take something from the till, one of the openers in the morning would get in trouble for the numbers not matching up. It wasn't just hurting my boss anymore. Other people are affected."

"Please, come with me to the police. They can keep you safe, and Jacob won't be able to hurt you anymore. He's not worth spending the rest of your life running." I reached out and gripped her hands, watching emotions flash across her face.

Finally, she nodded. Silently, she went into the back to wash her face while I tidied up her belongings in the front. While I waited, I texted Patel, letting her know I was bringing a witness to a crime to the station.

After a few moments, Stella came back out, her face freshly scrubbed, and her hair pulled back into a high bun. She looked like the Stella I remembered from the coffee shop.

"Will you drive?" she asked meekly. "I don't know if I can trust myself behind the wheel of a car right now."

"Of course." I guided her out of her house and into my car.

The roads were clear this time of day, and the sun had begun to poke its head out of the clouds. Stella's head rested against the back of the seat, her eyes shut, but a ghost of a smile was playing across her lips. She looked at peace.

Patel met us at the front of the station several minutes later and hustled us inside an interview room.

"It might be best if we talk alone," Patel said, glancing between the two of us.

"No, I want her here." Stella reached out and grabbed my hand. Patel and I exchanged a glance, and I shrugged.

We couldn't tell the poor woman she had to do this alone, could we?

Patel settled us into the interview room, Stella turning down an offer of coffee or water. Slowly, her voice low and her gaze down on the table, she took Patel through what she had told me earlier, adding in more details as necessary.

I watched Patel as Stella spoke, noting the way her face went from stern concentration, to shock and amazement, and back, as Stella described what she'd been doing for the past few months. Patel had a few follow-up questions for her, but mostly, Stella spoke. I shifted in my seat, the uncomfortable chairs making my back hurt more, and tried to focus on the confession in front of me.

After nearly an hour of back and forth, Stella sagged in her seat, her hands gripped in her lap, her statement finished. Patel made some notes on her notepad, then stood.

"I'm going to call someone from Victim Services to meet us here, then I'd like you to sign a statement attesting to all of this. Once we have your signed statement, we can put out a call to bring in Jacob for questioning. I need you to start thinking about where he might be right now." Patel cut her gaze over to me. "Simone, do you mind stepping outside for a moment?"

I followed Patel out of the room, squeezing Stella's shoulder as I went. Shutting the door to the interview room softly, I waited in the hallway while Patel spoke to someone quickly on the phone.

"Thanks, let me know as soon as you get here," she said into her phone, then hung up and turned to me. "Well, I gotta say, this was not at all what I expected when you said you had information about a crime."

"Trust me, it wasn't what I was expecting, either. I went

to her house to accuse her of killing Gayle, and instead, she tells me about this other crime she's been committing. It was a shock to us both."

"I'm going to ignore the fact that you just said you went to accuse a potential suspect of murder and instead focus on the fact that you helped close a case," Patel said, her eyes hard but a smile tracing across her lips. "Cuppa Joe's owner, Miguel, he's made reports about the stolen money but didn't know who was doing it. He's an idiot for not thinking to check the last person who handled the money each day, but if he'd done that, then Stella might be in jail while her boyfriend ran free."

Patel's phone buzzed again, and she answered the call. "All right, I'll be right there," she said after a moment. She hung up and turned to me. "Victim Services is here. We're going to keep Stella safe while we find her boyfriend and figure out exactly what happened. Thank you for convincing her to come and talk to me. You did good here." She reached out and squeezed my arm, then turned to go meet Victim Services at the front.

I watched her walk away, not quite ready to go back into the room with Stella yet. I knew I should stick around and make sure she was okay, but I needed a moment to myself. I'd saved her from an awful situation and was going to get her the help she needed, but Gayle's killer was still out there.

Stella had been acting strange because she'd been stealing from her employer, and I didn't think she was likely to come down to the police station if she'd murdered Gayle. Was it possible her boyfriend was involved with Gayle's death? Did Gayle learn about the stealing, and so he had to deal with her?

Once Jacob learned that Stella was talking to the police,

he was probably going to leave town as soon as he could. I wasn't interested in confronting a thief, so hopefully the police would find him quickly, and we could figure out whether he was involved in Gayle's death and Justin's attack or not. For now, I wanted to help Stella.

21

It was dark by the time I got back to my apartment. I'd stayed with Stella through the night, making sure she answered all the police's questions and that they didn't get too aggressive with her. She was still scared, but she understood the importance of what she was doing. Plus, she didn't seem too upset about throwing her boyfriend under the bus, which was understandable. He'd made her do some truly awful things!

By the time I'd left the station, the police had put out a warrant for his arrest and were combing through his personal and financial records to see where he may be headed. Stella squeezed my hand as I left, her cheeks tear-stained but her eyes bright. She'd done a good thing tonight.

The hallway was quiet as I climbed the stairs to my apartment. Normally, I could hear televisions playing from other apartments through the walls, but all was silent tonight. I glanced at my watch, my eyes bugging out at the sight of the time: 1 a.m. I guess that was why it was so quiet —everyone was asleep!

Thank goodness I'd dropped Lola off with Nadia at the

inn earlier today. After it had become clear at the station that I wasn't going to be home any time soon, I'd sent Nadia a text asking her to take Lola home for the night. I'd stop by Nadia's place early in the morning to pick up Lola.

I unlocked my front door, entering the dark apartment. I was back to square one with the investigation, with the two doctors currently at the top of my suspect list. Did I believe Liam and Deborah's alibis? They both seemed solid on the surface. An art show with hundreds of guests, plus a conference with many other doctors and cameras pointed straight at the cars in the garage. It'd be hard to fake that.

Of course, Deborah could've snuck away for an hour, or Liam could've found another way back to Pine Brook. You had to wonder, if their alibis were this good, had they been fabricated in some way, simply to look this good?

I shook my head to clear my thoughts. Patel had undoubtedly run down both alibis already; maybe, if I brought her a cupcake and a pitiful face, she'd share what she knew with me.

I stepped into my apartment, feeling my shoulders relax as I thought about tumbling into bed. It was way past my bedtime and I'd been up early that morning to get to the hospital to see Justin. The pain pills I'd taken that morning had worn off, and I hadn't wanted to take anymore while I was with Stella at the police station. I hoped a good night's sleep and a hot compress would help with the pain.

My gaze landed on the lamp sitting on a small table next to the front door. Hang on. Hadn't I left that on earlier today? I'd had a feeling I might be out late, and I liked coming back to a light burning. Had I forgotten to flip the switch?

I paused, shifting my attention to the rest of the apartment. All was silent. I must've forgotten to switch on the light. Nothing was wrong.

Just as I was about to turn the light on, I heard it.

A scratch, coming from inside the apartment. No, not a scratch—a shuffle. Like the sound you might make if you were sneaking along the carpet and didn't want anyone to hear. My floors were hardwood, but I had rugs strewn about the apartment so Lola wouldn't slip around.

My breath left my body as I tensed up, my senses on high alert. I wasn't alone.

My eyes flicked around the room, darting into dark corners. The front door led directly into the living room, with the kitchen and additional bedrooms further back. The floor-to-ceiling windows against the far wall let in the moonlight, though the place was dark. My eyes hadn't adjusted to the dark, so all I saw were shadows.

And then, it happened.

A figure stepped out from the hallway. Tall, dressed in black, face covered. My stomach clenched, and my mouth went dry as my brain struggled to comprehend what I was seeing. It felt like I was trying to pull my thoughts through mud, scrambling to understand what was happening in front of me.

Something flicked in the figure's hand, and I jerked, my gaze dropping down. They had a knife in their hand. The moonlight flashed off the blade. They took a step closer to me.

My body clicked into action at the sight of the blade. I let out a scream, so much louder than I thought I could, and turned, fleeing back through the door I hadn't fully shut behind me.

And promptly smacked into another person in the hallway.

"Simone! Slow down! Are you all right?" Nick gripped my arms, keeping me from falling to the floor.

I looked back over my shoulder, the entrance to my apartment dark and quiet.

"We have to get out of here," I managed to sputter out, my heartbeat pounding in my ears. I grabbed Nick's hand and dragged him down the stairs to the lobby and then out the front door of the building, ignoring his protests and questions.

"Simone, slow down! What's going on?" He gripped my hand tighter once we were outside, pulling me close as I shivered at the drop in temperature.

I looked back at the apartment building, waiting for the figure to emerge through the doors. But all was silent. Was the killer waiting for me inside?

"We need to call the police," I said, never once looking away from the building.

∼

"No one's inside," Officer Scott called as he emerged from the apartment building.

I let out the breath I hadn't realized I'd been holding. It was half an hour later. Nick and I were huddled together near the entrance to the apartment building, watching the police work. They'd shown up quickly once I explained what had happened on the phone, their screeching sirens waking the neighbors.

Other residents in the building had come downstairs to see what all the hubbub was about, some rolling their eyes and heading back inside once they saw me standing outside. Guess they weren't too worried about another body or crime scene I'd potentially stumbled onto, since it happened pretty often. Of course, this wasn't a body—this was attempted murder.

Scott came over to Nick and me, flipping open his notepad to a clean page. His eyes had heavy bags under them, and he looked ready for a nap.

"Take me through what happened here, please," he said, his pen poised over the page.

I explained that I'd gotten home late after helping Stella at the station and entered my apartment. I'd noticed the light wasn't on, which caused me to pause in the entryway, and that's when I'd heard someone inside. They'd stepped out from the shadows holding a knife, and I'd bolted into the hallway.

I paused when I got to the part about running into Nick, turning to him. "Why were you in the hallway? It's pretty late. I'm surprised I ran into anyone."

His cheeks turned pink, and he darted his eyes away from mine. "I couldn't sleep. One of my windows looks out over the parking lot, and I saw your car pull in. I wanted to make sure everything was okay since you were out pretty late, too, so I came to your apartment."

He looked back up at me, a small smile playing across his lips. My heart swelled at the realization that Nick had wanted to check on me to make sure I was okay.

Officer Scott cleared his throat, pulling our attention back to him. "And that's when you called the police?" he prompted.

I nodded. "Yes. Well, first we came out here. I wanted to get away from that person as quickly as I could. We haven't left this door, but no one went past us."

"We think he escaped through the back entrance. We found markings on your lock where it was picked. We're guessing this guy got inside and locked the door so that you wouldn't be suspicious, then waited for you to come home. Then, once you fled, he must've left through the back door. There are a few cars parked along the street back there; we're guessing his was one of those."

A chill went through me at the thought that someone had been waiting for me inside my apartment. Thank goodness I'd left Lola with Nadia today. What might've happened to her if she'd been inside when this person showed up?

"You keep saying 'he,'" I said to Scott. "Do you think the intruder was a man?"

His eyebrows raised slightly, then his face settled back into neutral. "Well, you tell me. You're the one who saw the perp."

"I'm not so sure." I thought about Deborah. She was tall. So was Liam. Currently, those two were at the top of my suspect list.

I shook my head. "It was so dark inside. I couldn't tell much. They were tall, but they were too far away to tell if they were a man or a woman. It might've been a man, or a woman wearing a thick coat. It all happened so fast."

Scott scribbled down a note. "Could you tell ethnicity or race?"

"I didn't see any skin. Their whole face was covered, and they were wearing gloves. All I saw was the knife." I shivered again as I pictured the blade flashing in the moonlight. Nick slid his arm around me, pulling me close.

Scott made another note in his notepad, then flipped it shut. "If you think of anything else, please give us a call. I'd suggest adding a deadbolt, too." He gave a curt nod and then left us to talk to one of the other officers onsite.

"Are you going to be okay tonight?" Nick asked once we were alone. "I've got a spare bedroom if you don't want to be alone tonight."

I hesitated. I was still grappling with my feelings about Nick after his girlfriend had shown up at the inn. Had I misunderstood the situation? My pride wouldn't let me open up to him about what was going on in my head, but I really didn't want to be alone right now. I didn't think the killer was likely to come back, not after all the police activity, but I didn't want to take that risk.

Instead, I simply nodded, and Nick led me upstairs to his apartment.

"There's an extra blanket in the closet if you get cold," he said, standing in the doorway to the spare bedroom. It was nicely furnished, and the bed looked comfy. I'd stopped off at my apartment to grab a set of PJs, and I couldn't wait to pass out on the bed.

"Here." Nick slipped his hand into his pocket and pulled something out, holding it out to me. It was his grandfather's Higonokami knife.

"For good luck," he clarified, taking my palm and pressing the pocketknife into my hand, curling my fingers around it. "You don't want to show up to another knife fight without a knife, right?" he added, a lopsided grin on his face.

I let out a bark of laughter. "No, I guess not. Hopefully, I'll only need this for luck and not self-defense." I slipped the knife into my pocket, my hand warm from where Nick had held it.

What exactly did it mean when a guy gave you a knife?

"Just call out if you need anything. I'm a light sleeper." He smiled, then took a step closer to me. He reached out to my cheek, cupping my face with his hand. "I'm glad nothing happened to you tonight." His voice was soft and low, and I couldn't stop myself from leaning into his hand.

"Goodnight." Then he was gone, shutting the door behind him, my face still warm from where he'd held it.

My body sagged, exhaustion coursing through me. I changed quickly, then passed out on the bed, barely remembering to take off my shoes first.

22

The next morning, I woke to a strange ceiling. The blankets around me were warm, and I considered burrowing down under them to go back to sleep. Then, the events of the previous night flashed before my eyes, and I shot up in bed, wincing as my back cried out in pain at the movement.

I was in Nick's spare bedroom. The clock read eight-thirty. I didn't know what time he woke up, but I needed to get out of here. I couldn't believe I'd let myself sleep in his bed while his girlfriend was staying at my inn. I quickly changed into my clothes from the night before and crept out into the hallway.

His apartment was silent. In the kitchen, I found a note from him on the counter.

I had to go to the farm early. There's coffee if you want it. Be safe today.

I crumpled up the note, then went to my apartment to shower and change clothes for the day. I'd been scared the night before, but that didn't mean I could suddenly start trusting him. Honestly, I was also ashamed of myself for not talking to him sooner about what was going on. I wanted to trust him, so badly, but my pride wouldn't let me open up to him.

Right now, I had other things to worry about.

My apartment was quiet when I entered it. The police had turned on the lights when they'd done their search last night, and I'd forgotten to turn them off. Not much had been disturbed. Whoever had been here to hurt me must've waited around for me rather than going through all my belongings.

This clearly wasn't a robbery. My heart skittered in my chest at the violation. Someone had waited for me in my apartment without my consent. Would I ever feel okay coming back late at night again? I shivered and shut the door quietly behind me as I left.

I headed straight for the inn, seeking solace after the invasion last night. I always felt Aunt Sylvia's presence when I was at the inn, and I hoped to get more of that comfort right now.

Nadia had brought Lola in for the day, and the beagle greeted me when I arrived. We walked into the bistro so I could grab a cup of coffee, and I spotted Miles sitting alone at one of the tables.

"Hey, how are you?" I asked, approaching his table. Lola hurried to his side and began licking his outstretched hands.

"What's wrong?" I asked as he looked up at me, his face forlorn and nervous. "Did something happen with Estelle? Do the police have her?"

"No, no, nothing like that," he said hurriedly. "It's just..." He looked up at me, then down again. "Have you talked to Estelle recently?"

I thought over the past couple of days. "We spoke briefly

yesterday, but just about a suspect. I've been a little busy looking for Gayle's killer. You won't believe all that's happened. But, wait, why do you ask?"

He sighed and stared down at his hands. "I don't know what's going on. She's not acting like herself. Everything was fine until Gayle turned up dead, and now...she won't talk to me. She's been acting strange ever since the police discovered that her pills killed Gayle. I don't believe she's a murderer, of course not. She's my wife," he said quickly. Was he trying to convince me or himself? "But I think she's hiding something. Do you think you could talk to her? See what might be wrong?"

"Of course," I said, leaning down and giving him a hug. "I'm sure it's nothing. She's just upset that her pills were used to kill someone, but I bet that's it. I'll go talk to her now. Is she at your home?"

Miles nodded. "I thought I'd give you two some space and go visit Lola. I think I'd like to take her on a walk, if that's all right with you?"

"Of course! I think she'd be very happy about that."

Lola had understood the word "walk" and was already running around the bistro, eager to go outside.

"I'll let you know if I find out anything," I said. Miles gave me another hug, then left.

I went into the kitchen to grab a cup of coffee. Estelle didn't need to see me half asleep. While I poured myself a mug from the coffee pot on the counter, I thought about my friend.

After learning that her pills had been used to kill Gayle, she'd seemed very upset, but I had to agree with Miles—she wasn't a killer. This wasn't guilt over what she had done. But was it guilt over something else? What was she keeping from her husband? Would she even tell me?

We'd only known each other for a few months, and while we'd gotten into some dangerous situations together, that didn't necessarily make us close enough that she would reveal something to me that she was keeping from her husband. I had to try to get her to talk to me, though. Miles was my friend, too, and I hated to see him upset like this. I wanted to do what I could to help them.

I FOUND ESTELLE AT HOME. She let me in, but I could tell she was upset, as she wouldn't look me in the eye.

"Tea, dear?" she asked, turning her back on me and walking into the kitchen. I followed, assuming she'd make me a cup regardless of how I answered. She was working on autopilot.

The kitchen was in shambles: dishes piled in the sink, dirty towels stacked on the island, a half-eaten soggy bowl of cereal sitting out. I stopped in my tracks at the door to the kitchen, taking everything in. I'd only ever known Estelle to be tidy and fastidious. This was quite a departure from her normal tendencies. I slid onto a barstool and kept my hands in my lap while Estelle made me a cup of tea.

"I figured out what was happening with Stella," I said after a few moments of silence. If Estelle didn't want to say anything first, I could. "You know how she was acting so weird after Gayle's death? Well, it wasn't because she killed her. She and her boyfriend had been stealing from Cuppa Joe's, and Stella was worried the police would figure it out."

There was no response from Estelle, who kept her back to me as she made the tea. I went on.

"Turns out, her boyfriend was forcing her to do it. I found her packing a bag about to flee town to get away from him. She told me everything, and I convinced her to talk to Patel. It doesn't sound like she was the mastermind behind this, so the police will probably want to go after her boyfriend. Isn't that wild?"

Estelle was silent. The only sound that could be heard was the stirring of the spoon as she added sugar to my tea.

"The killer was in my apartment last night. They threatened me with a knife."

Estelle gasped. "Are you okay?"

"Yes, I'm fine. But clearly we're getting close to the truth, if they'd come after me like that."

"Yes, I guess so." She kept her gaze on the mug in front of her. Where were all her questions? The Estelle I knew would have a million things to say after that bombshell. What was going on with her?

I sat forward, exasperated. "Estelle, what's going on? Why won't you look at me?"

She jolted out of her trance, turning around quickly and sloshing some tea onto her hand. I stood with a gasp and grabbed a towel from the counter, rushing to her side and wiping up the hot liquid. I carefully took the teacup from her and set it on the table, passing her the towel to dry her hands.

"Sorry about that. I'm a little jumpy today," she said with a weak laugh, her movements jerky and unnatural.

"What's wrong? You seem...odd."

"Oh, it's nothing," she said, waving her hand nonchalantly. "Just tired. Did you need something in particular, dear?"

"I spoke with Miles. He's worried about you. What's going on?"

Estelle's eyes flashed, but she didn't say anything right

away. "Nothing. I'm just tired, like I said. Miles has nothing to worry about."

"Does this have to do with Gayle? Do you know something about what happened to her?"

"I don't know anything about her death," Estelle said sharply, straightening up and glaring at me. "It's ridiculous that anyone would think that I did."

I held my hands up in a placating gesture. "I'm not accusing you of anything. I know you and Gayle were close at one point; is that what this is about? Are you upset that she died without giving you the chance to apologize for those things you said to her all those years ago?"

For one split second, her face opened up, and raw emotion shuddered through her. For a moment, she looked almost ready to cry. But then, as quickly as it happened, her face went blank and then hardened into a stare.

"I don't know what gave you the right to go sniffing around people's lives like this, but it needs to stop now." Her voice had taken on a tone I'd never heard before, and I shrank away involuntarily.

"You have a nasty habit of pushing your way into other people's business," she went on. "I've put up with it in the past because I thought it was charming, but now I see it's actually a menace. You're not a police officer, and you're not a detective. Quit nosing around my life before I tell Patel that you're going to ruin her chances of finding Gayle's killer."

I sat back, my mouth open, her words stabbing me in the heart. "Estelle, what are you saying? You were the one who convinced me to do this in the first place when we started snooping around Bethany's murder last year. And now you're saying I should stop?"

"You've clearly worn out your welcome. This town didn't

need an amateur sleuth before you came here, and we definitely don't need one now." Her gaze was hard, her tone emotionless. "I think you should leave now."

I opened my mouth, trying to think of a response, then snapped it shut. I wasn't going to get through to her now, not like this. I didn't want either of us to say anything else we might regret, so I stood and walked out of the kitchen.

She followed me to the living room and out onto the porch. As I turned around to say one last thing, she slammed the door in my face.

I couldn't just leave like this. She wasn't a killer, but she was clearly hurting about something. However, if she wouldn't talk to me, I couldn't make her.

I pulled my jacket tighter around myself, the chill in the air mingling with the chill I'd felt inside. I half-ran to my car, wanting to get out of here as soon as I could.

Her words had gutted me more than I wanted to admit. I'd thought I was trying to help her, but instead I'd just made her mad. After the break-in last night, I didn't feel comfortable in my home, and now my best friend was trying to hurt me. What else could go wrong?

I ARRIVED AT THE INN, shaking off the rain from my jacket as I entered the building. Someone had started a fire in the fireplace, so the lobby was warm, a nice change from the cold and stormy weather outside. The lobby was quiet. The only sound that could be heard was the crackling of the wood in the fireplace, so I went to the front desk to see who was checking in or out next.

I couldn't get Estelle's words out of my head. She'd never spoken to me like that before. She was obviously upset about Gayle's murder and was hiding something from her husband and me. More than likely, she'd need a couple of days to calm down and then would tell us what was going on. As far as I knew, she could be doing that right now with Miles.

Still, it hurt to hear what she had to say about me. She'd always treated me like a friend, a confidante, a daughter even. To have that taken away and have our friendship thrown back in my face like it didn't mean anything... It was a tough pill to swallow. No pun intended.

Of course, I wasn't going to let her harsh words stop me from finding the killer. This investigation wasn't about Estelle anymore. It was about finding the person who had harmed Justin and who'd invaded my personal space last night. I couldn't let that go, and their threats had only made me more motivated to uncover the truth.

"Simone, are you all right?" A voice crashed through my thoughts, pulling my attention back to the lobby. Nick stood at the front desk, concern etched across his furrowed brow and dark brown eyes.

I stood up straighter, pretending to read something on the computer on the desk in front of me, even though the screen was blank. "Nick. Hello. I didn't see you there."

"Yeah, no kidding," he said with a chuckle, though his features still held onto their concern. "I've been calling your name since I walked into the inn. Sorry I missed you this morning. How are you doing after last night?"

"Fine. A little tired, but nothing I can't handle." I smiled, typing a few keys on the keyboard so I wouldn't have to look him in the eye. "Thanks again for helping me out last night." My cheeks were warm as I remembered the way he'd cupped my face last night.

"Of course. I'd hate for anything to happen to you. I

hope you're doing okay." A blush spread across his cheeks as he spoke, and he looked down at the counter between us.

"Everything's peachy," I said, my voice taking on a cheery edge. "Well, I mean, there's still a killer out there, but nothing I can't handle."

Why was I acting like this? He'd helped keep me safe last night—I was sure that his presence had convinced my attacker to flee the building—so why wasn't I more appreciative of his help?

Because of his girlfriend, that was why. Maybe she was his ex, maybe she wasn't, but I was embarrassed about the whole situation and the way I'd trusted him. Still, I couldn't seem to find the words to explain myself.

He didn't say anything for a few seconds, studying my face. I squirmed under his gaze, keeping my eyes on the computer screen or the desk, anywhere else but his eyes.

"How's Estelle?" he said finally. "The police don't still suspect her of murder, do they?"

I shrugged. "I don't think so, but they don't really tell me much. They haven't brought her in for more questioning, at least."

"Is she around?" Nick glanced around the lobby. "I want to check on her, let her know I've been thinking about her. It's all such a tragedy, what's happened."

"I'm not sure if she'll be by today," I said. After her outburst at her home, I had a strong feeling Estelle wouldn't show up to the inn for a while. If she did, she was cockier than I realized.

"Oh, well, if you see her, will you let her know I'm thinking about her? And if she needs anything at all, just let me know. I don't know much about murder investigations, but I can make her a tasty cobbler," he added with a grin.

I returned a half-hearted smile. "I'll be sure to let her know. Thanks for stopping by."

Nick didn't take the hint to leave and continued to study my face. Was he trying to read my mind or something? His gaze was unnerving. I shifted my weight between my feet and focused on the computer screen in front of me.

"Simone, what's wrong? You've been acting weird for days. Is your back still hurting you? I know the doctor's office is probably pretty hectic right now, but if you need to go back to see a doctor, I can give you a lift—"

"It's not that," I interrupted. I sighed. May as well get it out there. Everyone was being honest today, weren't they? "It's just... Your girlfriend's here. She's been looking for you. There's nothing wrong with you having a girlfriend, of course," I added hurriedly. "She just caught me off guard when she showed up. I'm surprised you haven't talked to her yet."

"Girlfriend?" he asked, his face scrunched up in confusion.

"Simone." Tracy's voice came from the other end of the lobby. Our heads swiveled in her direction.

She took a step closer to the front desk, glancing between the two of us. "Can we talk in the back?" she asked me. "Nadia is going to stop by in a few minutes to keep an eye on the front desk."

"Okay," I said with a nod on autopilot. I turned to Nick. "I have to go." I slipped out from behind the desk and walked towards Tracy, trying to keep my steps steady as I did.

What had he been about to say? Why didn't I tell Tracy to give me a moment so he could keep talking? All these thoughts rushed through me as I followed Tracy to the back office. Would I get a chance to talk to him again?

23

I rubbed my hands over my face as I entered the back office. I was incapable of having a normal conversation with anyone these days. Were Tracy and I about to get into a big fight, too? She'd been absent for a few days, dealing with a family emergency, and I didn't know what she wanted to talk about now that she was here.

With my hands over my face, I didn't spot the person sitting in the office until Tracy introduced her.

"Simone, this is Isabella Rodriguez," she said.

My eyes flew open and landed on the person sitting in the chair across from Sylvia's antique desk. She stood as we approached, holding out her hand for me to shake. This was the woman who had come by the inn earlier this week, who I'd dumped that soapy water on and who wanted to talk when Tracy was back. Today, she was in a red pantsuit that looked more expensive than my rent, her hair pulled up into a chignon.

"It's wonderful to finally meet you," she said, a Spanish accent marking her words. "Tracy's told me so much about you."

I shot my gaze over to Tracy, a question on the tip of my tongue. Tracy stepped forward and motioned for us all to sit. She'd pulled two chairs behind the desk, so she and I now faced this Isabella woman. What was going on here?

"I'm also so pleased to finally get the chance to see more of the Hemlock Inn," Isabella Rodriguez went on, her gaze scanning the room.

Her eyes landed on one of the glass jars full of rocks Aunt Sylvia had collected from the beach. I wanted to stand up and protect the glass jar, but I held my seat. Just because my defenses were up didn't mean this woman was actually a danger. I was just feeling antsy after everything that had happened to me today.

"I've looked at pictures online, of course," she continued. "But it's so different seeing it in person like this. You can really tell that a lot of love has gone into this place."

"I'm sorry, I'm a little confused," I said, finding my voice. "What exactly are you doing here?"

Tracy turned to me, her eyes wide. "You didn't get my email?"

"What email?" Since when did Tracy email me?

Tracy looked back at Isabella. "I'm sorry about this, just a little miscommunication on our end. Isabella here is interested in investing."

"Investing in what?"

"Oh, well, the Hemlock Inn, of course," Isabella said with a tinkle of a laugh. "I would've thought that was obvious, but I do apologize for any confusion. I own a group of inns and bed and breakfasts up and down the West Coast, and I'm always looking for new opportunities to breathe life into tourist towns. When I heard about the Hemlock and this quaint little town you've got here, I had to come see for myself."

"Wait, so you want to give us money?" None of this was making any sense, but I couldn't tell if that was because it actually didn't make sense, or if I'd been so caught up in the murder investigation these past few days that I'd forgotten what it meant to be a business owner. Investors were a normal thing, right?

"Why were you here last week when I..." I didn't finish the sentence, remembering how much I must've ruined her nice outfit. Fortunately, Isabella had the good grace to smile.

"Yes, you really made an impression that day. I'd heard about the Hemlock and wanted to come see it for myself before reaching out. I wanted to see what kind of place it was. Even after our little mishap, I was interested in what you're doing here. I found Tracy's email on the website, and we set up this meeting."

At least my clumsiness hadn't turned her off of the inn. Still, I had so many questions, and I turned to Tracy hoping she could clear things up.

"I think maybe Simone and I should have a chat about this before we have this intro meeting," Tracy said, breaking in. "Why don't we plan to talk again this weekend?"

Isabella smiled and stood, reaching out to shake our hands again. "I'm looking forward to our partnership. Please let me know how I can help speed things along."

With a final smile, she left the room, leaving Tracy and me to stare at each other in silence.

"Are you okay?" she asked finally, moving to sit in the seat vacated by Isabella. I followed her lead and took a seat behind the desk. "You seem more...spacey...than normal. Is your back still bothering you?"

"No. I'm just trying to catch up with everything. Why would you set up this meeting without talking to me first? I thought...I thought you were trying to undermine my authority. I am the owner, you know." The words rushed out of me, my cheeks warming as I admitted my insecurities. Tracy needed to know how her actions made me feel.

"I would never do that! I sent you an email with all the details. Didn't you read it?"

I shook my head. Ah, that might explain why I had no idea what she was talking about. I wasn't the best at keeping up with my email, it was true.

She reached out and squeezed my hand. "I would never try to undermine you like this. You're a fantastic owner, and all I want to do is make this place better. When I heard from Isabella, I thought it would be a great opportunity for us to expand the inn. Together. I figured an investor could help us make those improvements we've been talking about, you know? Fixing up the rooms, repainting the walls, adding a bar to the bistro. In fact, with all the land around the inn, there might be ways to expand into a spa, or stables, or whatever we want!"

My eyes widened as I imagined her ideas. This inn had always been a quaint business in town, attracting a respectable number of out-of-town visitors and appealing to many townspeople with the bistro. I'd considered adding a spa at one point, but the money just wasn't there. With an investor, though, if we could add new services to the inn, that would draw in more visitors... The possibilities were endless.

"Why didn't you just talk to me about all this? Why would you send an email? We never talk over email."

Tracy shrugged, sitting back in her seat and crossing her legs. "You were out sick because of your back, then we had that busy weekend, plus you found another dead body, remember?" She smirked as she spoke. "It was never the right time, but Isabella wanted to come see the inn, so I figured an email was as easy as anything. I would've called while I was away, but I dropped my phone into some water, and I couldn't send text messages. I was able to send a couple texts at first, but then it shorted out, and I could only get into my email. I didn't realize you were one of those people who don't check email."

I sneered at her, though I couldn't stop the smile from spreading across my face. Yes, I was one of those people who had ten thousand unread emails in my inbox and only glanced through them when I was looking for a specific email. This wasn't the first time I'd missed an important email from someone.

"I'll make a note of that," Tracy said when I didn't say anything in response. "I'm always in my inbox, but I know not everyone is the same."

"Tell me about this Isabella woman." I leaned forward in my seat. "How did she learn about the inn? She seems much too glamorous to spend time in a dinky town like Pine Brook."

"That's what I thought too, but then I started looking into her. She married Enrique Rodriguez when she was young. You know, the hotel guy? He had all these hotel chains across the U.S. He passed away a few years after they married, and Isabella, rather than sell off his empire and live peacefully on the money, got strategic about it. She'd always preferred smaller hotels, B&Bs, that kind of thing, so, rather than get rid of all the hotels, she sold off the largest ones and used the profits to begin investing in smaller establishments up and down the coast. She gradually got rid of all the bigger hotels and now focuses on these individually-owned businesses. And she doesn't buy them up herself, but she'll pump money into them and help the owners turn a major profit, which in turn comes back to her."

This was almost too good to be true. It wasn't the first time someone had expressed interest in the Hemlock, and I had to wonder if we should be worried.. "How is she different from Tony Vasco? I thought we agreed that selling to him would've been a bad idea."

Tony Vasco had made an offer to my aunt before she died, and he'd made the same offer to me when I first came to Pine Brook. However, after falling in love with the Hemlock, and realizing that I could, in fact, run a business, I'd turned down his offer. His slimy sales schtick had also turned me off.

"She's nothing like Vasco. She's the real deal. I know some of the other inns she's invested in, and I reached out to a couple of their owners. They all said she was a lifesaver, turning things around for them when they thought they might have to shut down. It seems like she's now focused her attention on establishments that are already doing well rather than resurrecting a failing business. So, the fact that she's expressed interest in the Hemlock seems like a really good sign to me. She wouldn't be interested if she didn't think we could make her money back tenfold."

"Maybe..." It did all sound too good to be true, but Tracy wasn't easily convinced of anything. I'd tried to get her to agree to replace all the wallpaper in the rooms last month, and she'd responsibly turned down the idea because we couldn't afford it. She'd do her homework with Isabella and make sure this was the right decision for us. Still, it was a lot to take in, and it felt like my mind was running behind on everything.

"I know this is a lot to dump on you," she said. "Obviously, you need to agree to anything before we do it. Isabella's not in a rush, so why don't you take a little time to think it through? Read my email, and we can talk about it."

"That sounds like a good idea. I'm not immediately opposed to the idea. I just need some time to process it."

"Of course, take your time."

We chatted for a few more minutes about inn business. I pulled up Tracy's email and started skimming through the information about Isabella. It did seem like a pretty great offer. It also felt good to know that Tracy hadn't been trying to undermine me by bringing in an investor, but rather that we'd simply had a missed communication. I'd spent so much time feeling anxious about my relationship with Tracy and what all this meant, when I should've trusted that she would always do what was right for the inn, including keeping me involved in everything.

"By the way, how's Estelle?" Tracy asked after a few moments of silence.

I grimaced. "About as well as you'd expect. We, uh, had a little argument earlier. She's stressed about Gayle's death. I think she's keeping things from Miles, and it's just not good. But I don't know what to do about it. I've tried to find the killer, but it feels like everyone had a reason to kill Gayle. I thought maybe it was Stella, from Cuppa Joe's, but that's a whole other story. The receptionist from the doctor's office has been missing for a few days, and both doctors might've wanted to hurt Gayle. I just can't figure out the truth."

"Receptionist? Are you talking about Maria? I saw her in town earlier."

"What? Are you serious?"

"Yes. I guess it was near the doctor's office, but I think she was heading home. We didn't talk or anything, but it was definitely her. She's been missing?"

"Well, maybe not missing, but I talked to her after Gayle's death and she got all weird on me, then she left suddenly. No one's heard from her since, and I don't know if the police have had a chance to question her again. I thought she'd run out of town, possibly because of guilt."

"Well, she's definitely back. Maybe you should go talk to her now."

Even if I couldn't get Estelle to tell me what had made her so upset, maybe Maria could clue me in on what was going on with her and who might've killed Gayle. I wasn't going to sit around and do nothing while the killer was still out there, not after the attack on Justin and the invasion of my home. This was bigger than Estelle's secret.

24

By the time I finished all my work at the inn, it was too late to go see Maria. I was worried she would leave town again, but I also didn't want to bother her this late in the day. She was clearly back in town and not trying to hide her presence, which made me more confident that she would most likely still be around tomorrow. I wanted to get a good night's sleep and catch her early in the morning, before she had a chance to go to work.

Early the next morning, I went to Maria's home and knocked on her door. Was it a mistake coming here? If she had killed Gayle and hurt Justin, would she do the same to me? Should I have told the police what I was doing? Before I had a chance to fully process what I was doing, the door swung open, revealing Maria on the other side.

She gave a startled gasp and jumped when she saw me, then went to shut the door quickly. However, I moved faster than her and managed to stick my boot between the door and doorjamb.

"Maria, please, I'm just here to talk," I said, my foot

wedged in the space, keeping her from shutting the door. She deflated, her energy gone, and held the door open for me.

I stepped into her home, and she shut the door behind me. All the blinds were closed, so the rooms had a dark glow about them. The front door opened to her living room, which was cluttered but clean. Maria stepped away from me, clutching her hands nervously in front of her, her eyes darting about the room.

"When did you get back?" I asked, stepping into the living room.

"Yesterday afternoon," she said, her voice soft. "I-I was going to go to the police, but I had some things to take care of here..." Her voice trailed off, and her gaze fell to the floor. I followed her eyes and spotted a cat on the ground.

"This is Marty," she said, leaning down and scooping the cat into her arms. I reached over and scratched under the cat's chin, listening to it purr. "He's not mine, not exactly, but I feed him, and he always comes back to me. I needed to make sure he was okay."

"He's beautiful." He was sleek and black, with piercing green eyes that latched onto mine and wouldn't let go. "I heard you left town. Did you have a family emergency?"

"After we talked that day at the clinic about Gayle, I got a call from my sister in Seattle when I got home. Her daughter had gone into labor, and my sister needed someone to watch her other granddaughter while her mom was in the hospital, so I went up to help my family. A baby boy was born on Thursday, seven pounds, three ounces." She pulled her phone out of her pocket and swiped to a photo, passing it to me.

A frowning newborn stared up at me from the photo, his

eyes wide. Babies always looked like aliens to me, but I kept that thought to myself and passed the photo back to Maria.

"Congratulations."

"Look, you have to believe me. I didn't do anything to hurt Gayle," Maria said. "I didn't like the woman, but I wouldn't kill her."

"Yeah, she was pretty gruff. I heard her yelling at you that first day I was at the clinic to deal with my back. Do you mind if I ask what that was about?"

"Oh, it's just awful!" She collapsed onto the couch, Marty flying out from her grip once he got the chance. The cat strolled over to me and wound its way around my ankles. Lola was not going to appreciate his smell on me later.

"Just tell me what's going on," I said, taking a seat in an armchair across from her. Her hysterics seemed over the top, but clearly she had something to share. "If you didn't kill Gayle, then you have nothing to worry about."

She sniffled and wiped at her face with a tissue, blowing her nose. "Do you know about the annual pie contest Pine Brook puts on every year? It happens in the spring, so I guess you probably haven't been here for one yet."

I nodded. Hank had mentioned something about it a few weeks ago. He'd already started to perfect his pie recipe to enter it into the contest this year. In years prior, he'd wanted to participate but didn't think anyone would believe that a busboy could make a good pie. Since becoming chef at the bistro, he'd felt it was his chance to enter. I was looking forward to all the pie I'd get to try in a few months.

"Gayle and I always entered every year," Maria went on. "Some years I won, other years, it was someone else in town. Gayle never won. It was a friendly competition, even if she would say some rude things to the other participants. No one paid her much attention, though. Until last year. I...I was at the store, buying my groceries, and I...I picked up a pie crust...and Gayle caught me!" She let out a wail and buried her head in her hands.

I waited for her to go on. "And?" I said after a moment, when all she did was cry.

Her head shot up. "Don't you see? She was going to tell everyone!" Maria let out another wail.

Another beat passed, and she still didn't say anything else. "I'm sorry, I don't think I understand. What does your pie crust have to do with anything?"

"It was store-bought! That's against the rules! Gayle saw me, and she said she was going to tell everyone! I don't even normally use store-bought crust, but I was really busy around the contest last year, and I didn't have enough time. Do you know how long it takes to make a pie crust?"

I shook my head. We'd left my areas of expertise a while ago. "So, wait, let me make sure I understand this. Gayle saw you buy a pie crust from the store and was going to tell everyone you used store-bought crust for the pie contest?"

Maria nodded, tears streaming down her face. "All my friends would feel so betrayed. Everyone loves my pie, and if they thought I'd used store-bought pie in prior years, I'd lose my medals! Gayle thought this would be her chance to win if she could get me eliminated from the competition. I begged her not to say anything, I promised I wouldn't use the crust, and I even pulled out of the contest last year, but she wouldn't listen. She just wanted to win, and she was going to hold this over my head as long as she could." Maria continued to sob, her shoulders shaking from the effort.

"Maria," I said after a few moments of her tears, my voice gentle. "It's not as bad as you think."

Her head shot up. "It's worse than I think! It's awful! If everyone knew what I was planning on doing..."

"You might get eliminated from the contest, but your friends wouldn't hate you. Why didn't you tell me about this when I first came to talk to you? I've spent the last couple of days seriously wondering if you had anything to do with Gayle's death, and I know the police have been wondering, too. Why didn't you tell us the truth?"

"Oh, I couldn't bear it. I didn't want anyone to know what I had done. Once you started asking questions, I worried that the truth would come out, and then everyone would hate me. All my previous pie entries would be flagged as against the rules. I got called away to help my family, so I thought everything would quiet down here. Then I heard about Justin..."

I leaned forward and grabbed one of her hands, giving it a squeeze. I tried to keep my voice gentle, even though inside, I was flabbergasted as to how this grown woman could get so upset over pie crust. Clearly, I'd never entered a pie baking competition before. Next time Hank brought it up, I'd give it the respect it deserved.

"Maria, listen to me. You are not a bad person. I realize you didn't kill Gayle, and I'm sorry for thinking that. But I need your help now. You saw her every day and you worked closely with her. Can you think of anyone who might've wanted to hurt her?"

Maria let out a shuddering breath, trying to regain her composure. "I've been thinking about that, too. You don't get killed for no reason, right? But Gayle was mean to everyone. It's hard to think of someone in town who wouldn't want to hurt her."

I decided to switch tracks. "What about the doctors?

What did they really think about Gayle? I've talked to them both, but they didn't have much to say."

"What?" Maria recoiled. "You think one of them killed her? I don't believe it!"

I put my hands up in a placating gesture. "I didn't say that. But you have to agree that her killer was most likely someone she knew. How else would they have gotten the pills into her coffee? Plus, they would've needed to know about her allergy and what pills Estelle took. Both Liam and Deborah were aware of her allergy and could get access to Estelle's supplements."

"Dr. Bennett and Dr. Li never would've hurt Gayle." Somehow, Maria was more offended that I was accusing the doctors than she had been when I accused her of murder. Loyalty can make us do some very strange things.

"Look, I'm not trying to get anyone into trouble. I'm just trying to understand Gayle's life and who might've wanted to hurt her. Did the doctors ever say anything to you about how they felt about Gayle? I know she was difficult to work with sometimes. Did they seem to mind that?"

Maria shook her head and crossed her arms, shutting down. "No. I won't talk to you about them. They had nothing to do with this, and it's ridiculous to even suggest as much. I think you should leave now."

"Please, Maria, I'm just trying to find the truth—"

"Leave."

Her tone was final. I wasn't getting anything else out of her. I sighed and stood, giving Marty a scratch on the head as I walked out of the living room. Maria trailed after me and slammed the front door behind me. That was the second time a door was slammed in my face recently. Lucky me.

So much for my suspicions about Maria. Her motive was

weak and, even though she'd shown me anger when I questioned her bosses, she didn't seem to have the strength to have planned a murder and attacked Justin, especially since she'd been out of town when Justin was attacked. She'd given me nothing useful about Liam or Deborah, which meant they both stayed at the top of my list of suspects. And I was back to square one. Again.

25

I drove back to the inn, turning everything over in my mind. Maria was off the suspect list, as her reasons for killing Gayle were pretty weak. Plus, she'd been out of town when Justin was attacked. The police would be able to easily confirm her alibi, so why lie about that? I made a note to tell Patel what I had learned so that the police could check with her family.

Stella had been acting shady for different reasons and, now that she was with the police, revealing all about her crimes, it wasn't likely she'd had anything to do with Gayle's death. And, even though I'd gotten into a fight with Estelle and she was clearly hiding something, I didn't really believe she killed Gayle. She'd have to be very stupid to use her own pills to do it. Estelle was many things, but stupid was low on that list.

If appearances were to be believed, Justin had tried to kill himself because he had killed his mother. However, he'd come to me wanting to share information about the real killer. Why would he do that and then confess to killing her himself? He was still in a coma at the hospital and unable to speak, so we weren't going to get any answers from him for a while.

Which left Liam and Deborah. Both had access to Estelle's supplements, and both would've had the opportunity to mix them into Gayle's daily cup of coffee at the clinic. Both admitted that she was hard to work with, and Deborah even admitted that she was keeping something from Liam that she didn't want to get out.

But would she kill Gayle because she had threatened to tell Liam that she wanted to leave the practice? Why not just tell Liam what her plan was? She'd have to eventually, and killing Gayle would just muddy the waters. Unless, of course, there was some other reason she didn't want Gayle talking to Liam about her.

What about Liam? He was charming and kind, and Gayle seemed to really like him. Had things turned sour between them? Did he have some secret he didn't want the rest of us to know? Had Gayle discovered something about him which led to her death?

I pulled into the inn's parking lot and switched off the engine, but I didn't leave the car yet. Estelle's words were still running through my head. Was I wasting my time trying to solve crime in this town? I'd started looking into Gayle's death to help my friend, but if she didn't even want my help anymore...was it worth it?

Still, Justin was in the hospital because of this person. He'd wanted to do what was right for his mom and share what he knew, and someone had tried to kill him for it. This wasn't about Estelle anymore; this was about finding Justin's attacker and stopping the person who'd violently invaded my personal space.

In the lobby, Lola greeted me at the front desk. Nadia was helping to check in a guest, and I joined her behind the counter while she finished up.

"Long day?" I asked, noting that her energy levels seemed low.

She waved a hand flippantly. "Aren't they all? No busier than usual, but we're pretty busy these days. It's a lot to get through on my own."

I winced at her words. "Isn't Tracy around? I didn't realize we were leaving you alone."

"I think she had some paperwork to handle in the back. It's okay. I know we're pretty cash-strapped. Obviously, I'd love to have some help out here, but I get it."

"I'm sorry. I can take over here for a little while if you want to take a break?"

"Thank you!" She dashed off before I had a chance to finish my sentence.

Standing behind the front desk for eight or ten hours a day was a lot of work. Nadia always put on a happy face, but I knew it wasn't easy. We'd been able to hire more help in the past couple of months, but it still wasn't enough.

Isabella Rodriguez popped into my head. If we took her offer of investment, we could get more assistance for the front desk. But was I willing to give up some control of the inn? Was that the right idea? What would Aunt Sylvia do in this situation?

"Simone? Can we talk?" Estelle stood several feet back from the front desk, her hand rested on the chair in the lobby.

I didn't even hear her come in. "Of course we can talk, but I have to stay here while Nadia is on a break. What's on your mind?"

Estelle looked uncomfortable, wringing her hands in front of her. Was she here to apologize or to yell at me again?

"Listen, I'm sorry about what happened before. I didn't mean what I said, and it was wrong of me to even bring any of it up. I know you're just trying to help find a killer. I was the one who first asked you to look into this, and it was wrong of me to try to get you to stop."

"I appreciate that. I'm your friend, Estelle. But I can't take the lies."

She hung her head. "I know, you're right. I'm lying too much."

"Just tell me what's going on."

"All right." She took a couple deep breaths, then launched into her story.

"I know I told you that Gayle and I were friends when I first moved to town and that we stopped being friends after I made some comments about her parenting style. That wasn't the truth. She wasn't upset about any comments I made about Justin, but she was upset once she learned something about my past. It changed everything in our friendship. I don't want it to change the friendship you and I have, which is why I lied at first."

"Estelle, you can tell me. I won't think any less of you. You'll always be my friend, no matter what you did."

She took a couple deep breaths, steadying herself. "Years ago, before we came to Pine Brook...I cheated on Miles. It was a brief fling, and it didn't mean anything. At the time, Miles and I were living in Seattle. We'd been trying to have kids but it wasn't working, and I was feeling so emotional all the time. I met someone randomly one night, and I made a mistake with him."

My mouth dropped open. My thoughts flew to Miles, sweet, compassionate, caring Miles, who loved this woman more than life itself. But my heart also broke for this younger Estelle who'd always wanted to be a mother and was clearly struggling so much all these years ago.

"I know what you're thinking," she said, studying me. "I know what I did was bad. I don't even know how to explain it. But it didn't last, and I ended things as soon as I realized how wrong I was to hurt Miles. Gayle found out, though."

"How? If it happened before you came to Pine Brook, how did she even know?"

"I slipped up. I was feeling emotional and thinking about those kids we didn't get to have. Gayle was struggling with Justin, and we were trying to comfort each other. I wanted her to know that I also struggled in life, so I told her what I'd done. I didn't want to hide this from her. But she'd always hated liars and cheaters. She couldn't believe what I had done or that I was keeping it from Miles still. Things had been tense between us since then. Liam is a great doctor, so I still see him whenever I can, but I always hated that I had to talk to Gayle while I was there. She'd make little remarks, always thinking she was better than me. But she never told Miles the truth."

She squeezed her hands together in front of her, tears streaming down her face. I came out from behind the front desk and pulled her into a hug.

"I don't think any less of you. We all make mistakes. You've had so many good years with Miles, this was just a tiny error."

"I know what happened in your last relationship when that man cheated on you. I didn't want you to think I was as bad as he was, so I kept this from you. When Gayle died, I thought my secret would be safe, but then you were asking all those questions...I didn't know what to do."

"Gayle insinuated there was something in your past between the two of you. It's like she wouldn't leave it alone, she had to leave all these secrets around."

"Do you think that's what killed her? She had a secret about someone else, and they decided they couldn't let her live while she knew?"

"That would make sense. Maybe it was something she knew for a long time, but then everything came to a head recently, and the killer realized they had to kill her."

Estelle straightened up, like a lightbulb had gone off in her head. "I always worried she'd spill the beans about my affair to someone; maybe the killer decided they didn't want to take that risk with whatever secret she had on them."

"You might be right. Let's think about this logically. Where did Gayle spend most of her time? At work, or at home. Justin is currently in the hospital after being attacked by the killer, so it isn't likely that he killed his mom. That leaves work. I talked with Maria." I quickly explained her store-bought pie fiasco.

Estelle thought for a moment, back in her investigator-mode. "Hmm. While I do understand why she got so scared about Gayle knowing—these pie contests are pretty aggressive sometimes —it's a pretty weak motive. Still, I understand her fear. Gayle could be a pain in the butt when it came to town competitions like that. If she knew something about Maria that would disqualify her from the pie contest and embarrass her in front of all her friends, I can see why she'd get so upset about that."

I still couldn't see how it a pie contest made people so dramatic, but I didn't say anything. "All right, so we acknowledge that Maria isn't a viable suspect, regardless of how embarrassing her secret is. That leaves the doctors. I know you think Liam couldn't have had anything to do with this—"

"Actually, I take all that back," Estelle said. "Well, not all of it, but I realized how silly it was of me to think that he couldn't be involved. I mean, think of all the other murderers we've found in this town. I've been surprised by every one of them."

"It still brings up the question of motive. Why would either of them have wanted to kill her?"

"Maybe something strange was going on at the clinic. Gayle might've learned that they were doing something illegal and threatened to go to the police."

"What could they be doing, though? It seemed like an innocent enough setup."

Estelle furrowed her brow as she thought. "What about a pill mill?"

"What's a pill mill?"

"It's like a doctor's office that prescribes painkillers without sufficient medical history or information. Normally, you'd need to have a reason for getting painkillers, like a strained back, like yours. But at a pill mill, the doctor would prescribe the medicine without that history, in order to make money from the sale. They're essentially overprescribing opioids."

"How do you know all that?" I shook my head. "Never mind. Don't tell me." I dreaded the day that Estelle's internet search history was made public to the world. "Wouldn't they get caught if they were doing something like that? I can't see Maria going along with something like that."

"Not if they were careful. Maybe she had no idea what was going on. It might explain all the fancy clothes Dr. Li always wears."

"Her husband is a famous painter. He's got more than enough money for both of them."

"Okay, well, what about that poor woman who had a drug overdose recently? Where would she have gotten all the pills to OD? They could've given her too much, and so they had to cover their tracks. Maybe Gayle found out, and so they killed her to keep their secret."

"I asked Liam about that woman, and he said he didn't know her."

"Of course he'd say that, if they were actually running a pill mill! He wouldn't want to admit that connection. Gayle could've figured out what they were doing and threatened to go to the police, so they had to kill her to keep their illegal activities safe."

It wasn't the worst idea Estelle had ever had, but there wasn't much proof. We couldn't just go around accusing the doctors of running a pill mill without evidence.

I thought back to what had happened earlier in the week. "After I spilled my pills, I went back to get another prescription written, and Liam didn't want to give me more at first because he'd just given me some a couple days before. He kept saying how addictive they were. Why would he be so cautious if they were running a pill mill?"

"Because that other woman had just OD'd! And he didn't know you well enough to trust that you'd keep their secret."

"Hmm, I don't know about that...We don't have any evidence to bring to Patel."

"There's probably evidence at the clinic," Estelle said. "Let's go later, once it's empty, and see what we can find. There's probably some proof of what they've been doing."

"Breaking into a health clinic is a felony, Estelle! We could get in serious trouble for doing this."

"A woman is dead, and a young man is in the hospital! We must find the truth!"

I groaned, but I agreed with her. The police couldn't do anything about a supposed pill mill unless we had more proof. I wasn't eager to break the law, but this might be our only hope of finding the truth.

26

"You stay out here and call me if you see anyone show up, okay?" I said.

Estelle nodded, her eyes wide.

It was several hours later. Night had fallen, and we'd made our way to the clinic. We'd convinced ourselves the doctors were running a pill mill, and now we needed to find the truth, even if it meant committing a felony by breaking into a medical facility. Hopefully, we wouldn't get caught.

Estelle and I waited until it got dark before leaving the inn. We wanted to make sure the clinic was closed, and we didn't want anyone from the other businesses to see us sneaking around.

"How are we going to get in?" I asked her. "The first day I was at the clinic, I overheard Liam mention that the alarm was broken. Should we break a window?"

"Let's not resort to extremes. I can break the lock." She kneeled in front of the door and pulled out a small, black case from her pocket. She pulled out a couple silver tools and got to work on the door.

"Where did you learn to do that?" I said in amazement as she stood up a few minutes later, the door now open.

"I've been watching some videos online," she said, her smile proud. "You never know when lock-picking skills are going to come in handy!"

Every day, I learned more and more things about my friend that scared me. I pushed that thought out of my head and went to the front door. I had other things to worry about right now.

"Be careful," Estelle said, reaching out and grabbing my arm.

I looked back at her and smiled. "I will."

The clinic was quiet. I shut the door behind me with a soft click and paused to take stock of my bearings. I didn't hear anyone else in the building, so I began walking. I was a bit nervous about sneaking around a dark building after my recent attack, but I needed to do this to find the killer. Fortunately, my back wasn't bothering me too much right now. It was almost as if it knew I needed to snoop!

As I walked, I clicked on the penlight I'd brought with me to help me see. Turning on the lights inside would alert the neighbors that someone was here after closing, so I kept them off and followed the beam of my penlight.

Shadows danced along the walls. My footsteps echoed on the tiled floor in the hallway, and I took careful steps to try to lessen the sound. I pushed open the door to the waiting room and glanced around before stepping inside. It looked the same as it did during the day, but with more shadows hanging around. Old magazines lay scattered across the side tables and the TV was propped up in the corner, dark and quiet. The floor was carpeted in here, so I took hurried steps to get to the front desk.

Sliding behind the front desk, I settled into Maria's seat.

Her computer was dark and turned off, and I didn't know the password. Tapping a couple keys, the login page popped up. I sat back in the seat, thinking.

I typed in *Marty*, thinking maybe she'd used her cat's name, but that didn't work. Was Maria likely to make a really complicated password and change it every thirty days? Or was she the kind of person who would choose something easy that she could remember? Most people fell somewhere in between, but passwords were hard for everyone to remember. Maria might still write it down somewhere so she wouldn't have to remember it.

I lifted up the stapler, a candle, and a notepad, checking the undersides of these items, before finding a list of numbers and letters scrawled across the bottom of a Winnie the Pooh figurine. Gotcha!

The combination of letters and numbers written at the bottom of the list got me into the system. Someone would need to tell Maria she needed to do a better job of securing her password. That person would not be me.

Her electronic filing system popped up on the screen. I scrolled through the folders, but there was an extra layer of security to get into the patient files, and I didn't have those passcodes. I wasn't going to find proof of over prescribing pills on this computer, and my eyes were beginning to swim from the bright screen.

Logging off, I switched off the power again and sat back in Maria's seat, considering my options. I hadn't wanted to break in any deeper into the office, given the illegality of that. I'd hoped I'd find what I could on Maria's computer. Plus, I still pictured Gayle's body in the back room, and the rest of the clinic would've been completely dark. I didn't want to go sneaking around back there if I didn't have to.

But it looked like I was going to have to, as there wasn't

any evidence up here. I sighed and stood, switching my penlight back on and moving to the door that separated the waiting room from the rest of the clinic. I'd probably need a key for this one. Maybe Maria had one hidden somewhere.

The doorknob clicked open under my hand. I cocked my head to the side, furrowing my brow. That was odd. They didn't lock this door? I held my ear against the door, but I didn't hear anything on the other side. Glancing over my shoulder to make sure I was still alone, I slid open the door and slipped into the back offices.

With all the chaos of the murder investigation and the police in and out of here, maybe they'd simply forgotten to lock this door at the end of the day. They were down one nurse and struggling to keep up with all their patients. It made sense that some things would get forgotten. Still, they probably should've been more careful about security since one person had already been killed here.

I shut the door softly behind me and paused, straining to hear. Nothing. No breathing, no footsteps. I was alone. I continued down the hallway, running the penlight over the corners.

File cabinets were built into the walls, but they were all locked. This was probably where they kept the paper files for everyone. I wouldn't be able to break these locks, and it would take too long to go through every file to see if anyone was getting more pills than they were supposed to. I needed to find another computer with more information on it, so I kept walking. The first couple of doors I passed were exam rooms, quiet and dark this late. Not what I was looking for. I continued walking.

The next door I opened led to a more traditional office, with a large desk, computer monitor, and bookshelves lining the walls, filled with medical textbooks and reference books.

A photo of a smiling Deborah and her husband, Geoff, stared up at me from the wall. This was Deborah's office. Was she likely to keep her password written down on a Winnie the Pooh figurine? I doubted it, but I had to look.

I sat in front of her computer. A plastic mat was under the computer, presumably to protect the mahogany wood desk from any scrapes from the computer. I tapped a key on the keyboard to turn on the computer screen. A login page popped up. Drat. She seemed like the kind of person to come up with a really long and convoluted password. I wasn't likely to break into it easily. Maybe I should go looking in Liam's office.

I pushed away from the desk, my hand bumping against something shoved under the mat. I paused. What was this?

I grabbed the item and pulled it out, revealing a tan folder. It looked the same as the other patient folders I'd seen in the clinic, but why was it shoved under Deborah's desk? Was she trying to hide it?

I opened the folder and skimmed the first page. I wasn't an expert on patient files, but I'd assumed the first page would contain stats related to the patient—height, weight, blood pressure, etc.

This folder, however, contained notes. My breath caught in my throat as I read over the scrawled notes.

Patient shows signs of obsession...Patient unable to separate reality from fiction...Patient unlikely to keep our assignations a secret...

Who was this "Patient" the notes referred to? And what happened to them? What *assignations* had they had? I kept flipping through the notes, looking for anything that might help me figure out what was going on here.

The folder slipped from my hands as I landed on the last page. There was only a photo on this page, clipped to the back of the folder. A young woman smiled up at me from the image. The rest of the pages in her folder were scattered across the floor, but I didn't bother picking them up. I couldn't take my eyes off this woman.

Miriam had texted this same picture to me earlier in the week. Rebecca Hanlon, Patel's overdose victim, was a very pretty woman. At this point in her life, she'd added highlights to her hair and contoured her cheeks. I had to imagine that her last images, taken before she'd died, wouldn't be this beautiful.

A Post-it note had been attached to the bottom of the image. *Patient cannot reveal the truth.*

A chill went through my body as I finally recognized the handwriting, which I'd seen on a prescription made out for me. That was it. It all made sense. Patel's overdose victim, who was actually her murder victim, the notes in this file, the reason Gayle was killed. It was all because of the same person.

The door creaked open behind me, and I spun around.

"I really wish you hadn't seen that." Liam was standing in the entrance, gripping a heavy-duty hole punch. He raised it into the air, arching his body, then all went dark.

27

L ights pressed against my eyes. I opened one eyelid, then shut it as the brightness increased. My head pounded and my mouth felt dry like sandpaper. The pain in my back was almost unbearable. Slowly, I opened both eyes and held in the urge to puke. That wasn't going to get me anywhere right now.

I was on my back, closer to the ceiling than I would've been if I were on the ground. I blinked my eyes several times, straining to clear out the fuzzies. I took a few deep breaths, the smell of antiseptic and something else strong in the air. I heard footsteps in the room and the sound of shuffling papers, but I couldn't see anyone in the room.

I tried to sit up, but my arms strained against my sides. They were strapped down. So were my legs. Panic rose in my belly, up my throat, and a gasp escaped me. I was stuck here.

I could still move my head, so I turned it this way and that, trying to see what was going on. My vision blurred as I moved it, but slowly the darkness faded. My eyes landed on someone in the far corner, hunched over and messing with something on the table in front of them. They straightened up and turned around.

It was Liam.

My eyes filled with tears. "Please," I sputtered, my voice hoarse. "P-please let me go."

"I'm sorry," he said, keeping his gaze down. "I-I can't do that."

Shock recoiled through me. Gone was the charming doctor who'd wooed everyone in town. In his place was this...this shell of a man. He looked up at me, sadness in his eyes, then dropped his gaze again. In one of his gloved hands, he clutched a syringe.

"Please," I said again, my voice coming out stronger and louder this time as I regained my energy. My head ached and my back hurt, but I fought past the pain. "You don't have to do this."

"Oh, but I do," he said with a sigh, his gaze down on the syringe, which was full of a clear liquid. "You've shown that, by showing up here and sticking your nose where it doesn't belong. I don't want to, but I must."

He took a step closer to me, gripping the syringe tight. He leaned in and pressed it against my arm. Then, just as quickly, he pulled away.

"It's not right," he muttered, turning away and going back to the table he'd been standing at. "I need to find what's right." He set the syringe down. It clattered against the metal table, and he shuffled through some more instruments.

My stomach rolled as I heard all the tools he had lain out in front of him. What was he going to come at me with next?

"Please, just let me go. I won't tell anyone."

"I can't do that. I've made a mess of everything, and now

I must clean it up. I'm such an idiot. Why did I think I could do this? Liam, you're so dumb. Stupid, stupid, stupid."

He hunched over, gripping the table tightly as he berated himself. Where was this coming from? Who was this man in front of me?

"Liam, it's okay. Just tell me what's going on. Why did you tie me down?"

"Oh, you know way too much. I can't let you out of here."

"But I don't know anything! I was just looking around for Maria's bag." The lie was out before I realized what I was saying, but I kept it going. "She asked me to come get it for her, but I couldn't find it at the front, so I went searching in the back. I'm just here to get a bag."

He paused, considering my words, then his face crumbled again. "Stop lying! I know that's not why you're here! You figured out what I did, and now you're going to tell everyone. But I can't let you do that!"

He whipped around again, the syringe back in his hand. I had to keep him talking.

"Tell me what's going on. Who was that woman in the photo? Was she one of your patients? What happened to her?"

He paused, still hunched over, but he hadn't come any closer with his instrument. "That...that was Becky. She was so nice to me. I...I used to take care of her. I was helping her get better."

So then, how did she overdose? I kept my questions to myself. "Where did you meet her?"

"In town. We became friends. She...she wanted help. Her parents died in a car crash five years ago. She was in the car. She survived, but she had back pain ever since. She came to me, needing help. She was sick and she needed my help, so I helped her. I helped her so much. We were so close. But then...but then it all went bad."

"What happened? How did it go bad?"

"I gave her too much! I thought she could handle it, but it was too much. And then she was dead! I had to get her away, so I took her to the creek. But they still found her, and I knew they'd know it was me. How could they not? We were so close. But no one came for me. No one knew."

He shuddered, as if the energy of getting all these words out of himself was too much to handle.

I had to keep him talking. Estelle was still outside. She'd realize what was going on. How had Liam gotten past her? She was smart; she would've hidden herself when she realized someone was showing up. She wouldn't have let him see her and was probably calling the police as we spoke. I just needed to keep him talking.

"So the police never figured out what you did. I talked to Detective Patel, and she had no idea who killed Rebecca, I mean, Becky. So what happened? How did we end up here?"

"It was that nosy Gayle! She couldn't stay out of what wasn't her business. She overheard me on the phone with Becky. It was the week before...before Becky died. She was asking for more pills. I couldn't do it, though. I didn't want to. But she was desperate. I told her I'd bring her some that day. Gayle had come into the room when my back was turned. She pretended like she hadn't heard anything, but I knew she had. She had this gleam in her eye, and she asked about the call. I told her it was nothing, none of her business, but she wouldn't listen."

He'd started pacing around the room, but at least he was staying away from me with that syringe.

"What happened next?"

He paused, as if trying to find the words. "I went to

Becky, and I gave her the drugs. But it was too much this time, and she died." It was like he couldn't stop the words from pouring out of him, now that he had someone to confess to.

"Gayle must've realized that's who I'd been talking to on the phone when the police announced her death. She told me she was going to tell the police if I didn't confess. She said she hated liars, and that she couldn't work for one. But I wasn't lying! I was only trying to protect myself! I couldn't let her ruin things for me. I made a plan. I knew Gayle was allergic to those pills Estelle takes. I knew she and Estelle had a bad relationship, so people would suspect Estelle first. All I had to do was steal a couple pills from Estelle and drop them into Gayle's coffee. I didn't expect you to show up that day, but finding her body together was the perfect cover."

Anger coursed through me. This man was going to let Estelle rot in jail for something he had done. Any sympathy I had for him was gone, but I needed to keep him talking if I was going to get out of here alive.

"What about Justin? I know he didn't try to kill himself. He told me he had something to tell me, but when I showed up, he was dead. What happened?"

Liam's face crumbled. "I didn't mean to hurt him. He always liked me. He wanted to talk. He said his mom had told him I'd been keeping secrets, and he...he just wanted to know the truth. He didn't think I had anything to do with her death, but..." He paused, his gaze fuzzy.

"He must've seen something change in my face because, suddenly, he didn't want to talk. He told me he didn't know anything and that he was going to go home. But I couldn't let him go like that. Not after he suspected me. If he told the police about what Gayle had said, they'd be all over me."

"So what did you do?"

"I went to his house. I knew where they kept the spare key. I waited until it was almost dawn because Gayle always said Justin was a night owl. He would game all night long...I broke in, and I found a razor blade he keeps in the bathroom. I brought a bit of chloroform to knock him out, then I slashed up his wrists. It was so much easier than I thought."

A shudder coursed through me at the thought of what this man had done. I was strapped down, all alone, with a monster.

"I made sure to wear gloves, and I put his fingerprints on the blade so that the police would think he'd committed suicide. I didn't think you'd find him so quickly. I can't believe he survived." He broke down again, tears coursing down his face.

Is that why he was at the hospital that day? Was he trying to find some way to finish killing Justin? He hadn't thought anyone was around, and when he looked up at me that day, I'd seen real fear in his eyes. I was seeing this same man in front of me now.

This man was weak and scared, but he was also a monster. That was a horrible combination. I couldn't let him hurt me, too.

"I didn't want to do any of this," he muttered. "I just wanted to keep my practice and keep helping people. But they were all going to try to take this away from me. I had to stop them. And now you're trying to take my practice away, too. I can't let that happen."

I tensed up as he approached the table with the instrument. I couldn't die, not like this. How was I going to get out of here?

"Liam, you don't need to do this. If we go to the police together, we can tell them what happened. They'll understand."

I was getting desperate and saying anything I could think of to convince him not to come at me with that syringe. I imagined what might be in there, and what it would do to me if he injected me. Would it look like an overdose, like with Rebecca? Would he dump my body by the creek, too? Or would he bury me deep underground, never to be found?

He stopped and balled up his fists at his sides, his face scrunched up. "It wasn't supposed to happen like this! Everything was going fine! Then Gayle had to stick her nose into things that didn't concern her. I had no choice."

"I know you didn't," I said soothingly. If I could convince him that I was on his side and that I was not going to hurt him, maybe he'd let me go. "Everyone knew how awful Gayle was. She was mean to everyone! I'm not surprised she hurt you this way."

Liam opened one eye, looking at me. "Do you mean it?" His voice was soft and quiet, like a child's.

"Of course."

I tried to sit up, but the straps allowed me no leeway. Guess I was going to have to talk him off a ledge while strapped to the table.

"I know you didn't mean to hurt anyone. You didn't mean to hurt Becky. You were just trying to help her."

"I was." He spun around so he was facing away from me, and he began pacing the room again. "She was so sweet and kind to me. But she had a problem. I was only trying to help her, but it all just got out of control..." His voice trailed off as he stared down at the floor.

"Tell me about her," I said. Anything to keep him talking. "What was she like?"

His face lit up. "She was funny. She used to tell the best jokes. We'd laugh together all day. And she was beautiful. I used to take so many pictures of her when we were together. I never wanted to forget her face." His face scrunched up again, tears pooling in his eyes. "I had to delete all the photos after she died. I didn't want anyone to know we knew each other."

Just then, something clattered off a shelf in another room. Our heads shot up and swiveled to the door. Liam looked back at me, his eyes wide.

"Who's here?" he hissed, keeping his voice low.

"I don't know—" I started to say.

But he came over to me and smacked his hand across my mouth to keep me from talking. Darting his gaze around, he spotted something on the table and grabbed it. Suddenly, he was shoving a wad of gauze into my mouth. I gagged against the intrusion, but he didn't push it in so deep. Just enough to keep me from calling out.

He pressed his finger against his lips in a shushing gesture, then skulked over to the door and pressed his ear against it to listen. I couldn't hear anything over the thumping of my heart. He sent one glance my way, then clicked open the door and slipped into the hallway.

I relaxed against the table, relieved that he was gone. I tried to push the cloth out of my mouth with my tongue, but it wouldn't budge. How was I going to get out of here? I felt around with my fingertips, but my wrists were strapped down tight. His knots were strong.

I thrashed my body against the exam table, hoping to loosen the straps on my ankles. That's when I felt something in my back pocket. It was the Higonokami knife Nick had given me earlier! He'd been worried about my snooping around; who knew he was right to be worried?

If I could just get it out of my pocket, I could use it to set myself free. I wiggled around on the table, trying to reach it, but it wouldn't move. A crash came from the other room. I paused, straining to hear, but all was silent again. Who was out there? Had Estelle come inside looking for me? I renewed my energy to grab the knife from my pocket. I couldn't leave her out there to deal with Liam alone.

I flailed around repeatedly, my abdomen striking the table so hard I nearly knocked the breath from my lungs. The knife slowly inched up the pocket, poking into my waistline. One final smack and the knife slipped out of my pocket, landing on the table next to my hand. I reached over and grabbed it, flicking out the blade, and began working on my binds.

Several moments later, Liam burst through the door. I launched from the table, binds dangling from my wrists as I held the knife in front of me.

"Stay back," I ordered, planting my feet in case he decided to run at me and try to knock me over.

He hesitated a moment, then ran towards me with a shout. I stepped to the side, trying to get out of the way, and he smacked into the table. He grunted and grabbed my arm, trying to pull me to him. I kept my grip tight on the knife, slashing out at him. He jumped back, slamming his head into one of the exam lights he'd positioned over the table. He cried out, his attention now focused on his head. I reached out for anything heavy I could find. I grabbed a bed pan from the counter and swung it at him. The force of the hit knocked him to the ground, and he groaned.

I relaxed my stance and leaned back against the table, adrenaline still coursing through me, my back crying out in pain. I was finally free.

28

I made Liam walk in front of me as we left the room. I wasn't letting him get behind me ever again. As we entered the lobby, the front door burst open, and police officers streamed into the waiting room, their guns drawn. Estelle and Deborah brought up the rear, and I almost burst into tears of relief. I put my hands in the air, dropping the Higonokami knife, and waited for them to take Liam away.

After the police decided I wasn't a threat, I was able to go over to Estelle, who pulled me into a hug.

"I'm so glad you're okay!" she said, squeezing me tight. I held onto her like a lifeline.

"What happened?" I asked, pulling away and looking around. "Where did you go?"

"I was still outside, but I hid! I saw Liam slip into the clinic, so I waited a few minutes to see if you were going to come out. When I didn't hear anything for a little while, I called the police and banged on the dumpsters to distract him and give you a chance to escape."

"I was coming back to the office to pick up some things,"

Deborah said, inserting herself into the conversation. "I saw Estelle and asked her what was going on, and she told me what you two suspected. I know I wasn't running a pill mill, but Liam had been acting erratically recently. I thought something more might be going on. How did you get away from him?"

I pointed at the Higonokami knife. The police were currently bagging it for evidence. "A gift from a friend. I don't know what I would've done without it."

"So is it true? Do you really think Liam killed someone?" Deborah's eyes were wide at the thought.

I nodded. "He admitted everything to me while we were in the clinic. He said he gave those pills to that Rebecca woman who overdosed, and that he killed Gayle because she found out what he had done. He was going to silence me, too, if I hadn't gotten away. He had me strapped down to the table and was going to inject me with something." I shivered at the memory of that syringe.

"Wow. Well, I'm so glad you're okay," Deborah said. "I had no idea Liam had done any of this. He'd started to act a little weird after that first woman overdosed, but I thought it was stress. Then, when Gayle died, he threw himself into the work. I just thought he was trying to make up for the fact that we were down a nurse."

"What's going to happen with the clinic?" Estelle asked. "Are you still leaving town?"

"I don't see how I can now. This town needs physicians, and the hospital can only handle so many patients."

"What about Geoff's need to travel and go paint somewhere else?" I asked.

She waved her hand flippantly. "Why are his dreams the only ones that matter? He can paint anywhere. This town needs a doctor." She smiled proudly at that.

"The only reason I figured out what was happening was because I found a file on your desk for Rebecca Hanlon. I recognized Liam's handwriting in the file's notes, but why was the file on your desk?"

Deborah's eyes widened. "That little weasel! He was probably hoping to put the blame on me if the police ever came around with questions about her. That poor woman. He was just trying to cover his tracks."

"All right, someone needs to tell me what's going on." Patel interrupted our circle, her face stern.

"I should've called you earlier when I thought there might be evidence at the office," I said. I took her through everything: our suspicions that the doctors were running a pill mill, finding the evidence inside that Liam knew about that other woman, him showing up and knocking me out, then waking up strapped to the table.

"How did you get into the building? Isn't it normally locked?" Patel asked.

"Well..." I glanced over at Estelle, not wanting to admit that she'd been teaching herself how to pick locks.

"It's fine," Deborah said, holding her hand up to stop Patel. "Clearly, some locks were broken into, but I'm not going to press charges. These women have saved my clinic. They didn't do anything wrong in my book."

"All right, doctor. That's your choice." She turned back to me. "Your story is interesting, but Liam is out there claiming that you attacked him with that knife. He says the police arrived just in time to free him from you because you were threatening him with a knife."

"That's not true!" Estelle burst in. "He's been lying to everyone! The proof is in the clinic, I'm sure of it."

Apparently, Liam's defense mechanism had gotten rid of that weak man who had strapped me down, and now he was doing whatever he could to save himself. Would the police even believe my side of the story?

"Wait!" I looked up at the women in front of me, a smile blooming across my face. "He has photos of the woman who OD'd. He called her Becky. He said he deleted the photos from his phone, but nothing is truly gone from your phone. Pull his records from the cloud, and I'm sure you'll find them."

Patel considered me for a moment, then nodded. She turned to Deborah. "You worked most closely with him. What's your take on everything?"

"I know he's been lying about things. If Simone says he attacked her, then I think you should trust her."

"All right, we'll pull those phone records and see what we can find," Patel said with a nod. "I also did some digging into his alibi. He knew Gayle's death was an allergic reaction so fast at the crime scene, so I'd been suspicious of him from the beginning. Turns out, no one saw him for two hours at that conference he claimed to be at when Justin was attacked. We think he might've used cash to get a cab back to Pine Brook. That, plus your claim that he tried to hurt you, should be enough to get a warrant for his phone records. I have to go take care of a few things now, but, please, no more breaking into buildings." She left, pulling out her phone to put in a call for a warrant.

"I can't believe it's all over," I said to Estelle. "Honestly, after learning so much about Gayle, I can finally relate to her."

"What do you mean?"

"Well, she was nosy, right? She loved knowing secrets about other people, even if she wasn't actually going to do anything with them. She never went to the police with what she knew about Liam or about Stella. She just liked having her secrets. I can't blame her, since we're pretty nosy, too. She didn't deserve to die because of that nosiness."

"I guess you're right," Estelle said after thinking about it for a moment. "Wow, I never thought I'd find something in common with Gayle."

"I think it's time for us to leave. I'm looking forward to curling up with Lola and a cup of tea. Tonight has been too much to handle."

Estelle agreed, and we walked away from the clinic, the police lights flashing all around us.

THE NEXT DAY, I was back at the inn, sore from the events of the night before. Getting strapped down to a table and fighting with a man much larger than me had tweaked my back again, and I was still in some pain. Estelle had encouraged me to stay home for the day and rest, but I wanted to get back out and see people. Liam had taken away my freedom by strapping me down like he did at the clinic, and I wanted to break free and be around people again.

Fortunately, Deborah had given me some muscle relaxants, and my back was feeling so much better, even better than before. Deborah was clearly the superior doctor out of the two of them. I also felt much less jumpy now that I knew Liam was behind bars.

"I still can't believe it was Liam." Tracy shook her head as she passed me another finished gift bag for a wedding party that was arriving that weekend. I was glad they wouldn't be here while a crazed killer was on the loose.

"He hid the truth from everyone. He managed to look so charming and put together, but that facade was hiding a sad little boy deep down inside," I said.

"Have you heard any updates on Justin? Do you know how he's doing?"

I nodded. "I went by the hospital this morning before coming in. He'd finally woken up. I told him what had happened with Liam and his mother. He confirmed that he'd told Liam about what his mother had said, about Liam keeping secrets, and that Liam's face had changed right in front of him. That's when he realized he was the killer. He'd texted me as soon as he could, but Liam still had time to attack him. He's grateful I showed up when I did."

"How did you even get out of the clinic? Estelle said he had you tied up."

"Nick gave me a knife, actually," I said with a laugh. "I'd almost forgotten I had it on me. Without it, I wouldn't have escaped."

"Wow, that's amazing. He's a keeper." Tracy smiled. "I'm so proud of you for saving the day. I don't like the ways you get involved in all these murder cases, but you're making a big difference in this town. That's important."

"Thanks." I grinned. "Stella actually showed up to see Justin at the hospital before I left. I guess they've been talking. I think they might start dating."

"Well, at least someone in this town can have a happy romantic relationship. Have you thought more about the offer from Isabella?"

I nodded. "I have. I'm still a little wary, but if you think it's the right decision, then I trust you. Let's have another conversation with her and see what changes she suggests."

I'd been thinking about it all night and, while I was worried that we'd lose the essence of Aunt Sylvia if we made too many changes, I also knew that she had left us with the inn because she trusted our instincts. Isabella's ideas could help us bring in more money and allow us to pay our staff more, which they so desperately deserved. I was open to hearing what Isabella had to say.

After hurting my back again last night, I had to admit that it was okay to need help at the inn. Tracy was a great general manager, but if Isabella's investment meant we could hire more staff, it was the right thing to do for the inn. And then maybe Tracy and I could both actually take a vacation sometime.

"Agreed." Tracy looked up at the lobby, where someone had come down the stairs. She straightened up almost imperceptibly. "Well, speak of the devil."

I followed her gaze and saw Isabella walking towards us from upstairs. She waved when she saw us watching.

"Good morning, ladies," she said, her accent adding a nice feel to the words. "Can I just say, that bed is one of the best I've ever slept on. Nice job here."

"Thanks. I'm glad you could stay with us for a bit," I said. After her visit before, it made sense to rent out one of the rooms to Isabella so that she wouldn't have to leave town so soon, and it gave her a chance to experience the inn like an actual guest.

"I heard all about your antics last night," she added. "I hope you're okay."

"Thanks. I'm getting there. It's not my first time getting caught up with a killer, but hopefully, it won't happen again any time soon."

Isabella shivered. "I can't even imagine it. You must be so brave."

"Or careless," Tracy piped in, grinning. "But it's all right. We still like her."

The two women smiled at each other, sharing this private joke, and I glanced between the two of them. Was I seeing something here? An attraction I hadn't noticed before? Before I had a chance to ponder what I was witnessing, the inn's door blew open again, and Nick walked through.

I straightened up at the sight of him. I hadn't expected to see him so soon. I looked over at Tracy and nodded my head in his direction.

"I'm just gonna go say hello," I said, unable to hide the smile on my face.

She smirked. "As long as you do only that."

I left the two of them at the front desk, meeting Nick halfway through the lobby. He opened his mouth like he was about to say something, but I hurried in first. "Do you mind if we go talk in the courtyard?" I didn't add that I'd chosen it because it was private.

His smile was warm. "Of course. Lead the way."

We settled onto the settee, our knees almost touching. The courtyard was quiet, a bit chilly, but we were comfortable.

"How are you doing after your near-death experience last night?"

I took him through everything, including the little knife that had saved the day.

"Wow," he said once I was finished. "Who knew that little thing would save the day?"

"I'm forever grateful to it," I said. "The police are holding it as evidence, but Patel said I could come pick it up later today since Liam confessed to everything last night. Maybe you could come with me?" I'd realized that I'd been assuming the worst about Nick, and after his knife had saved the day last night, I'd realized that I could trust him. I just needed to open up to him first. He wasn't a bad guy like my ex, and I needed to give him a chance.

"I'd love to do that," he said, taking my hand and squeezing it.

I smiled. "Thanks for coming by today. I appreciate it."

"Yeah, I just wanted to apologize about everything. I've been such an idiot. I should've talked to you about that woman as soon as she got to town. She's my ex, though she doesn't like to think that's the truth. We've had some back and forth in our relationship. But I told her this time that things are over now."

"Wow. How did she take it?"

"About as well as you'd expect. Which means not great, but she doesn't really have a choice. I told her she needed to leave the inn and go back to Seattle. We won't have to worry about her anymore."

"We?" I raised my eyebrows in question.

Nick dropped his gaze. "I've been such an idiot. I don't know how to act around you half the time. I think you're so great, and I love talking to you. I don't want to mess up whatever we have going on here, but it's so hard to know what to do, and—"

He was rambling, and while it was cute to watch, it wasn't getting us anywhere. I leaned forward and cut him off with my lips.

This was a much better way to end a murder investigation. I'd have to keep it in mind for next time!

THANKS FOR READING!

If you enjoyed reading about Simone and the Hemlock Inn, I'd love it if you could leave a review on Amazon and Goodreads. Honest reviews of my books help bring them to the attention of other readers.

ACKNOWLEDGMENTS

A huge thank you to everyone who read the first two books and came back to find out what happened next with Simone and the town of Pine Brook. Thank you so much! If you enjoyed *Medicine and Murder*, I hope you'll help me spread the word about the series by telling your friends or reviewing the book. Those things really make a difference!

ABOUT THE AUTHOR

Josephine Smith is an author of cozy mysteries. A Washington state native, Josephine now makes her home in Northern California with her husband and dog and cat. She loves all things sweet, foods and people included, and can be found with her nose buried in a book. Visit her website at www.josephinesmithauthor.com, or connect on social media at Josephine Smith, Author (Facebook and Instagram).

Come say hello!

Made in the USA
Middletown, DE
14 October 2021